DIARY OF AN 8-BIT WARRIOR

FORGING DESTINY

Published in French under the title *Journal d'un Noob (Guerrier Suprême) Tome VI*
© 2018 by 404 éditions, an imprint of Édi8, Paris, France
Text © 2018 by Cube Kid, Illustration © 2018 by Saboten

Andrews McMeel Publishing
a division of Andrews McMeel Universal
1130 Walnut Street, Kansas City, Missouri 64106
www.andrewsmcmeel.com

19 20 21 22 23 SDB 10 9 8 7 6 5 4 3 2 1

ISBN: 978-1-4494-9446-9 hardback
978-1-4494-9445-2 paperback

Library of Congress Control Number: 2018952004

Made by:
Shenzhen Donnelley Printing Company Ltd.
Address and location of manufacture:
No. 47 Wuhe Nan Road, Bantian Ind. Zone,
Shenzhen China, 518129
1st printing—12/10/18

ATTENTION: SCHOOLS AND BUSINESSES
Andrews McMeel books are available at quantity discounts with bulk purchase for
educational, business, or sales promotional use. For information, please e-mail the
Andrews McMeel Publishing Special Sales Department: specialsales@amuniversal.com.

· CUBE KID ·

DIARY OF AN 8-BIT WARRIOR

FORGING DESTINY

Illustrations by
Saboten

Andrews McMeel
PUBLISHING®

We set out for **Owl's Reach**—the monsters, mysteries, and musty passages of the **Tomb of the Forgotten King** now behind us. As I fiddled with the squishy **glowmoss,** my mind wandered to **Urf,** to the **advanced crafting table,** and to the bizarre chain of events that had just occurred. Who could have guessed when I left Villagetown that I'd be fighting bosses with Breeze, **Pebble,** and some mysterious human?

Speaking of which, I **bombarded S** with questions during the whole way back to town. He seemed to know **just about everything,** so why **not?** Sadly, this little **interview** didn't go as well as I'd planned. His answers were from a **human's** perspective, which was confusing to a villager like me.

"Why is the sky blue?"

"Because Earth's sky is blue. The original game would have looked **strange** with, say, a **purple** sky."

"**Oh.** Why do villager boys have **big noses** while villager girls have small ones?"

1

"**Entity** was responsible for that, I think. He and a few others were working on a **new server mod** to make villagers **more lifelike.** This included villagers with different **personalities,** outfits, and **genders.** But after that, many of the players said the **girl villagers** looked strange, so **Entity** made their noses smaller and gave them hair. Then the **Scribes**—*a handful of players tasked with writing the history of the game world*—added a paragraph about how villager boys shave their heads as a **tradition.** And after the **server crash,** every last word the Scribes originally wrote **became real."**

"You lost me. What's this about the **crash?** What happened?"

He went on to tell me that, in the Earth year **2039,** their world was facing **imminent destruction.** As the final hour approached, some of them chose to flee into **VR,** or **virtual reality.** Apparently, all they had to do was throw on **a helmet** to be transported to another world. But that was just **imaginary**—an **illusion.** The world they had escaped to was this one—once known as the **Aetheria server.**

After having spent thousands of hours in **this virtual world,** most of them had made **countless friends,** and they wanted to say **goodbye.** They were all the most hardcore of **game addicts,** and they'd spent more time in Aetheria than their own reality. Not many of them even had **friends** in the real world. Some didn't even have **family.** So it was only fitting for them to spend their last moments in a world they cherished, **surrounded by <u>virtual friends</u>. . . .**

"So what happened?" I asked. "Your world **didn't end?** The real one, I mean."

"We have **no way** of knowing. With the countdown approaching zero, those logged in **lost consciousness** and eventually woke up in a different area—still logged in to the game. **And the game was different, somehow. Real.** We couldn't quit or exit. To this day, we're still able to access the original **main menu** system, but it's unresponsive."

"**Oh.**" I stared ahead blankly, until something **caught my eye.** "Hey, look! A coal vein! Let's stop for a bit and mine!"

S looked at me
<u>and sighed.</u>

By the time we hit **Owl's Reach**,
it was <u>**dark and cold.**</u>

A **chilly wind** blew through the streets. The place would have seemed **abandoned** if not for **those few** scurrying here and there.

Even so, most of the shops were **still open.** Their windows, glowing cheerfully in **the gloom,** flickered every now and then when there was

"Take care out there."

"Breeze. Runt. It's . . . been real. Stay safe."

"Thanks again. Couldn't have done it without you."

"Good luck on your quest. Be sure to visit us, 'kay?"

movement inside. But first we headed to the square with **our new allies.** There, we saw each other off.

I watched them go, **wishing** we'd said more than **simple goodbyes**—wishing we'd never had to say goodbye at all.

But they had **their quest,** and we had **ours.** Wind gnawing at our backs, the two representatives of **Team Runt** walked straight to that blacksmith. Or is it *Team Breeze* after today . . . ?

The blacksmith gave me **750 emeralds** for the glowmoss, as promised. We traded the loot for another ◆3,572. That was **unusual,** I think, because it was mostly **Urf's stuff,** not the boss loot. Breeze and I felt it'd be a **good idea** to give those items to our friends back home. Souvenirs from our **first little tour** of the Overworld. And if you were wondering, yes, Breeze **insisted** on keeping **that dumb stick.**

We went to the **Quill & Feather** right after the blacksmith.

After we **sauntered** in, I looked **Feathers** straight in the eye and slammed ◆2,500 onto her light-blue carpet counter. "I'll take an **advvvvvaeon** forge." *(Not a spelling error. I began to say "advanced crafting table" then smoothly transitioned to the item's real name. Because I'm as smooth as an ice block on a warm, sunny day.)*

"That was quick," she said. "You must have found **a quest.**" After glancing downward, and eyeing Breeze with **a knowing smile,** she added: "And by the looks of it, I'd say **your quest went rather well.**"

Huh?!

What'd she mean by that?!
And why does she keep staring at our hands?!

Only then did I realize that Breeze and I were . . . **uh . . . holding hands.**

Well, the wind was **freezing** tonight. It even felt cold **indoors.** So her hands must have gotten cold. These northern biomes, you see . . .

"**You've got it all wrong,**" I said. "She's not **my–**"

Breeze **interrupted** me with a smile. "Our quest **did go well,** but we're rather **exhausted,** so if we could just **get that forge . . .**"

"I'll be right back."

A minute later, I was holding **a cube of raw and unimaginable power.** It was **warm** to the touch, and its emerald-and-diamond grid **pulsed softly.** I found it hard to believe that this item was **thousands of years old.** It looked as though it had been **crafted** only yesterday: shiny,

6

its gray surfaces without a single **scratch** or blemish, the diamond emblems of tools adorning its sides showing **no sign of wear.**

I handed it to Breeze, who began carefully **inspecting it** like the **neophyte historian** she was.

"**Will that be all?**" Feathers asked.

*Like this thing isn't **enough!*** I thought. I gave her a nod.

As Feathers opened her mouth to deliver what I guessed was that **standard shopkeeper line,** I beat her to the punch, saying it **loud** and **fast: "PLEASURE** DOIN' BUSINESS WITH YA." *(Boom! She didn't know what to say to that! Only closed her mouth and slowly blinked. When it comes to dealing with these shopkeepers, I'm a pro.)*

After I pocketed the forge, Breeze dragged me outside by the hand.

"The mayor will be **thrilled,**" she said, as we both approached her horse.

"You don't think he'll be **mad at me** for taking off without speaking to him first?"

"No, **I don't think so.** Once he sees what you're carrying, I'm sure he'll lighten up. **My father, too.**"

"Yeah. You're right."

I felt such a relief.
My mission was complete.

All we had to do was hop into **Shybiss's saddle** and head back home. Well, maybe not right away: It was getting late, and we had more than **enough emeralds** to spare for another night at that inn. If we wanted, we even had enough to buy **a second horse** in the morning, **a breakfast fit for a king,** and about one hundred healing potions— because, like I learned today, you can **never** have **too many** ways to keep up your health.

I mentioned **my plan** to Breeze, who added taking **another hot bath** to the list. So with the forge tucked **safely** away in my inventory, we set out for a warm room, a warmer dinner, and **a sound night's sleep.** Shybiss was also exhausted by now, and the way she puffed with huge frozen breaths resembled **a redstone steam engine.**

8

When we arrived at the **Enchanted Dragon,** Breeze took Shybiss to **the stable** out back.

A few seconds after she left, I heard a loud **knocking.** This was followed by **a shout.** It was coming from **the other side** of the building. So hands in my ~~pockets~~ inventory, I took a little **stroll** in that direction.

This side of the inn, opposite the stable, had a small building attached, with its own door. It must have been **a side entrance** used by the cooks and other staff. When I rounded the corner, the door was **wide open,** and the innkeeper stood just outside with a waitress.

"I thought I told you **not to come back!**" the innkeeper bellowed.

"**Please,**" the waitress said. "I really need the work. Just give me one more chance."

"I've already given you **plenty!** How many times did you show up late? Often **dirty,** no less! Just as you are now!"

"I'm sorry, sir. I've been . . . working **a second job.** I need help," she pleaded, voice **trembling with despair.** "Please. It won't happen again. **I promise.**"

9

"Enough! I've already hired someone else. And before you **seek work elsewhere,** little lady, I suggest you learn the difference between a **stormberry roll** and an **enderpuff cake!**"

Upon unleashing this brutal criticism of her serving skills, the portly innkeeper stormed inside and **slammed** the thick spruce door. The waitress **slowly** turned around, head lowered and slight shoulders **sagging.** She **jumped** upon noticing me.

Her **golden hair** was tangled and damp, and her **uniform** *(one of the many elaborate and official outfits worn by servants in the Overworld's larger cities)* was **disheveled** beyond belief.

Her expression was in the same condition. It could only be described as worn. **Exhausted, worried,** and full of doubt. Looking at her, I couldn't imagine she'd spent the previous night anywhere except **out on the street.**

With a slight shiver, she made her way toward the front of the inn, **ignoring me** as she did. **But she didn't make it.** As though **dizzy,** she stumbled and **tripped** on a crack in the mossy cobblestone path, where she fell to her knees with a gasp. She **struggled** to pick herself up.

"Hey . . . are you . . . **are you okay?**" I asked.

"I . . . feel **kinda** . . ."

That was it. **She collapsed to the ground.**

"What happened to her?" Breeze asked. She was **right beside me** now—I hadn't even heard her approach.

"I think she's **sick.**"

The **poor girl** now appeared to be unconscious, mumbling **something about a quest.** As I studied her, I felt more and more as though **I'd seen her before.**

That hair . . . and that voice!
No . . . how is this . . .

Breeze **crouched down** beside her. "**That's strange.** Looks like she recently killed a slime." She pointed to **one section** of the girl's tunic. **A dark green patch.** The dried ichor of **a slime.** "What was a waitress doing **fighting . . .**"

Breeze **suddenly froze** when she realized who it was.

I'd already recognized her. The color must have **drained** from my face. I opened my mouth, but I couldn't make a sound.

Of course, we could have **identified her earlier** using **Analyze,** but we've only had this ability for less than a day, so using it **isn't instinctual** yet. When we did look up, it only **confirmed** what we already knew.

This was a girl **who shouldn't have been here,** let alone in those clothes or **this pitiful state.**

A girl quite famous for her bravery, compassion, honor, discipline, and skill.

A girl praised for graduating at the top of her class.

A girl who hailed from Villagetown.
A girl known as Ophelia.

The first thing we needed to do was to get Ophelia inside.

Although she wasn't seriously injured, she had three status effects: Exhaustion, Food Poisoning, and Chill. These were debuffs, the same kind as Mining Fatigue.

Her Exhaustion must have worsened over time, until finally rendering her unconscious. It was a huge stroke of luck that I was there right when it happened. If she'd remained outside, her Chill would've intensified in much the same way, until it led to something far worse than sleep.

"I've never carried someone before," I said.

"It's easy. You grab her shoulders, and I'll grab her knees."

"Okay. She's not so heavy, huh? Wait. How do we open the door?"

The front door swung open just as I said this. Two dwarves barged through. One of them eyed the unconscious Ophelia warily.

"That's the one who served me mutton instead of a pork chop," he muttered to the other. "And my stormberry roll was burnt!"

"Sounds like a villager, all right," the other said. "Those NPCs wouldn't know a **crafting table** from a **block of slime.** What's **with** all the villagers lately, anyway? **Where do ya think they're coming from?"**

I wanted to listen **further,** but Ophelia was getting heavy.

Nearly as heavy were **the innkeeper's eyebrows** as he glared at us from the counter.

Upon noticing that we were **carrying Ophelia** like a sack of beetroots, he **started yelling:** "What's she **gotten into** now? Forget it, **I don't care! Take her somewhere else!** I won't lose **any more** of my customers—they can't stand the sight of her!" He **glared** at her. **"Bad** for business, that one. **Never on time!** Always mixing up orders! I've had to give out over twenty **free** potions just this week!"

"We'll take a room," I said politely.

"Maybe you didn't **hear me,** little villager. **There are no rooms avail—**"

I handed off Ophelia to Breeze and *(politely)* slammed a shiny green pile onto the counter. "Like I said, **we'll take a room.**"

I have no idea **how many emeralds** I gave him. I wasn't counting. **Over three hundred,** if I had to guess. For **some** strange reason, **Theor the innkeeper** wasn't so angry anymore.

Just like the one from **the night before,** our room had only **two beds.** But that didn't matter: **We had that enchanted bed.** After placing it near the furnace, **we set Ophelia down.**

OPHELIA

The icon with **the moon behind a bed** is **Exhaustion.** If you stay awake for exactly **twenty-four hours,** you get **Exhaustion I.** This debuff gives a **small penalty** to most tasks, including **crafting,** movement, and ability use. **Exhaustion II** appears at **thirty-six hours,** and the penalties are **tripled.** Level III appears after **two whole days without rest,** and the result is the **loss of consciousness.**

The icon resembling **rotten green meat** is **Food Poisoning.** Some monsters, such as **husks,** are capable of inflicting this debuff. It's more likely, however, that Ophelia had consumed a **raw, poisonous,** or **rotten** food item out of sheer desperation. The duration of the debuff was **abnormally long.**

The heart encased in a block of ice is **Chill.** Like Exhaustion, it **hinders** almost every task. Some monsters—and, **according to Breeze,** several abilities—are **also capable** of inflicting this debuff. Yet there was no doubt in my mind that Ophelia got this by staying out **too long** in the cold.

(Note that even though her Exhaustion and Chill had an infinite duration, they could be removed through adequate sleep and warmth.)

Needless to say, this was the **greatest mystery** I'd encountered yet.

What happened to Ophelia? Why was she apparently **homeless?** Had she run away? Why had she been **fighting slimes?**

"We need milk," Breeze said. "**That will treat her poisoning.** The rest will just take time. Two hours, **three at most.**" She paused. "I forgot to bring a bucket."

"I'll go find one," I said. "You just **stay with her.**" It was my turn to pause—much longer than hers. "**Breeze?**"

"**Yes?**"

"Was she still in Villagetown **when you left?**"

"I can't remember," she said. "I was outside with **Emerald** and the others most of the time. I never saw her much after graduation. As far as I know, she was **with her own group.**"

"And you didn't hear anything about her?"

"**No.** Stump did say at one point that he missed her. He hadn't seen her much, either. They **danced together** at the party, remember?"

With a slight nod, I headed back out, **angry at myself** for not having the foresight earlier to buy **three iron bars.** I could have crafted a bucket myself. **Of course,** I'd still need a cow. And then there's the fact that I'm still not the best at crafting. The last time I made a bucket in class, **it had a hole.** I tried to convince the teacher that I'd done it on purpose. . . .

"It's the **Hole I** enchantment," I'd said.

"And what **redeeming quality** does it have?" Ms. Oakenflower had asked.

"Well, um . . . **convenience.** You see, you no longer have to tip the bucket over to empty it."

She'd **smiled coldly.** "Perhaps you could demonstrate this **enchantment** of yours for the rest of the class."

"Of course."

"Sorry, folks! As you can see, this enchantment still needs a little work."

"Our textbooks did need some cleaning, though."

Most of the shops were **already closed** at this hour.

On top of that, **the wind** had gotten **even worse.** It practically had a knockback effect, and **its howling** through the alleys is probably what **a ghast** sounds like.

When we were **riding** back earlier, S told us about **a ghost** that **wanders** this city at night. I **laughed** at the time—just another **legend.** But then, as I was walking alone, I totally believed it. There's just something **creepy** about **Owl's Reach** after dark.

I eventually found a general store that had what I needed.

With the bucket like an ice block in my hands, I made my way back **as fast as I could,** hoping I wouldn't **get lost.** And wondering if milk can freeze. **That was when I heard a cry.**

Don't worry—**it wasn't a ghost.** It was three young humans, all of them armored and brandishing swords. Their iron breastplates bore **the sigil of a red sword,** as though painted on. They were running through the streets and **looking down** every passage and alleyway.

"Where'd he go?"

"Curse his invisibility!"

"Look! Over there! I see him!"

All of a sudden, one of these men pointed his sword **at me.**

"You can't hide from us, **villager!** Return **that ring** at once, or be forever hunted by the **Solemn Blades!**" As they trudged in my direction, taking their time, I, **um . . .** well, I carefully **stashed the milk.**

What? It took me **forever** to get it, **okay?** I didn't want it to spill!

"What's your **problem?!**" I called out, drawing my swords. "I'm no thief! I didn't steal anything! Can't you see I'm just a **simple villager** doing my nightly milk run? You can't have a stormberry roll without **milk!** You just **can't!**"

One man raised an eyebrow. "What's he babbling on about?"

"Pay no mind," another said, peering into the gloom behind me. "Just some noob."

"It could very well be **a distraction,**" said the third. "They often work together. **Don't let your guard down, fools!**"

I had **no idea** what was going on. I backed up against the wall as they drew closer. Then I heard **a voice** less than two blocks to my right:

"Whaaaaat?! Runt, is that you?! What are you doing here?!"

"Oops! Gotta go! See ya later, **blockbrain!**"

I **barely** caught a glimpse of **who** had just spoken before he disappeared again.

"**There he is!**" shouted one of the knights. "**His invisibility is wearing off!**"

In a symphony of clanking and yelling, the knights **chased after him**, sprinting past me **as if I didn't exist.** The **shouts** and **insults** continued until one last cry echoed in the distance: "**Bat farmers . . . !**"

I stood there for a moment. **Without budging,** only breathing. I forgot about the cold. *Cogboggle. That was Cogboggle!*

What is happening?! Even though it was **dark,** and even though he was only there for a second after I looked, **that voice was unmistakable.** Cog has this **super annoying** voice, scratchy and **shrill.** It's not something you can easily forget.

I sprinted back to the inn with my thoughts swirling in my head.

Ophelia, Cog—why are they here?

One was a waitress. Another's robbing people blind.

Why? To what end?

I had this eerie **feeling.**
And as I ran,
the streets seemed to grow
darker and **darker.**

Breeze was still **tending to Ophelia** when I got back.

Through healing potions and food, she'd nursed the "**waitress**" back to full health.

She'd crafted the potions **herself** using ingredients traded in the dining hall. As for the food, she'd ordered it.

And **what splendid food it was!** Enderpuff **muffins.** Glazed **moonseed** cupcakes. And, of course, **the** most **magnificent** of all bread-based food items: **the stormberry roll.**

At the sight of all these **heavenly** pastries, all other thoughts more or less **flew into an ender portal.**

There are many different food items that include **stormberries** in their crafting recipe—biscuits, muffins, scones—but **the stormberry roll** is the easiest to craft, as well as **the most efficient,** since it requires the fewest ingredients per unit of food restored. Further, while cupcakes are best reserved for a sunny afternoon, or perhaps an extravagant party, the stormberry roll—with its **simple, understated elegance**—can be eaten with any meal, in any location, and under any circumstance. Whether you're **crawling** through a dungeon's sewers or attending the **wedding** of a prince, consuming a stormberry roll is **never** deemed inappropriate.

Truly, the stormberry roll is **the workhorse** of the pastry world. With a **subdued,** sweet taste and dark blue berries flickering with yellow swirls like lightning, this **humble pastry** will always be there for you when you need to refill your hunger bar. *(It also provides a slight buff called **Omnessence**, which lasts for one hour and increases experience points gained by 2.5%.)*

After biting into one of these rolls, the icon for **Omnessence** appeared in **my vision** like a little candle glow.

"You haven't eaten in **hours**," Breeze said, handing me another. "I'm **surprised** you could still sprint."

"Moommmrrrmmeeeeemrmrmrrraw."

"Uh, what?"

I wiped away some crumbs. "I **said,** you won't **believe** who I saw! **Cogboggle! He's here!** He **stole** something from this group of knights! The **Solemn Blades.**" *(I said this name in a ridiculously deep and heroic voice, because that was how they talked.)*

"Are you sure it was **Cog?**"

"You ever known another villager to call someone a **blockbrain?**"

"Err. **No.**" **She sighed.** "This isn't making any sense. **Why would they be here?** Do you think **Villagetown** could have been attacked?"

"I've been asking myself **the exact same thing.** But if it had been, I'm sure **Cog** would have said something, right? But he just **ran off.**"

"Whatever the case, I'm sure we'll have our answer **once she wakes up,** won't we?"

Breeze took my bucket and gave Ophelia **the milk.** The green icon vanished, and Ophelia's expression, pained up until now, was as **soft** as enchanted wool.

"She'll **recover faster** now," Breeze said. She set the bucket down next to the **Bed of Roses** and then flopped down onto her own bed. "But she still **needs sleep,** and so do we."

"**Yeah.** We're about to hit **Exhaustion I** ourselves. In other news, I'm on my **twenty-seventh** diary entry. What a **day,** huh?"

I turned
toward Ophelia.

29

I had a nightmare.

Villagetown was burning. Everyone was running for their lives.

No, **not everyone.** My friends were still there, **fighting valiantly.**

But it seemed as though they were **losing.** At least, **Kolb's sword** was **broken.**

Was this a **vision of the future?** Or was it already in the past? Or was it just **my own fears** inspired by Faolan's tragic tale?

It was **still dark** when I woke up. My armor slightly clanking, I went over to the window and saw that the moon was on its way down—two or three hours past midnight, roughly.

Breeze was sound asleep, as was **Ophelia.** But the waitress, now at **full health,** was stirring gently in her sleep. She didn't have any more **status effects.** I considered waking her up, but it seemed **a bit cruel,** given that her day yesterday seemed even worse than mine.

I stepped toward my bed but **stopped myself** immediately, because my armor sounded like a bunch of **pots and pans** clanking together. You know the sound an iron golem makes when it walks? **Yep. That sound,** pretty much, which was probably why Ophelia kept moving in her sleep.

*All right, you can do this. A **ninja** would have no problem moving silently in metal armor, even old rusty armor like this.* I did my best creeper impression, more or less **slithering** across the floor without a single clank. **Unfortunately,** Breeze had left that milk bucket in the shadow of Ophelia's bed. So, **of course,** I happened to **step on it.**

Clearly this made me **trip and fall** on it. And **naturally,** this sent the bucket flying into a wall—which **obviously** didn't stop there—and **clattering around the room** with a sound similar to a mine cart on powered rails. **Or two.**

That bucket just wouldn't stop rolling. First, Breeze **shot up** in bed and **scrunched up** against the wall. Then I heard a door creak open in the hall, followed by **muffled shouting.** Only then did Ophelia stir in her bed once more and **rise slowly** with a yawn.

OPHELIA

GOODNIGHT BUFF.

23:59:19

She looked **so confused.**

I mean, imagine: She wakes up in **some random room,** with me,
a villager wearing **ridiculous armor** and a hat **covered in mold,**
staring at her while a bucket won't stop rolling around on the floor—all
of this along with **some dwarf shouting** far away down the hall,
whose words are only partially comprehensible but clearly not very nice,
stuff like **"slime-loving"** and **"what in the frozen Nether?"** repeated
over and over.

Ophelia tilted her head. **"Runt?** Is that you?"

"It is," I said, stopping the bucket with my foot. It made one last
little squeak.

The waitress looked down at herself. **"What happened to me?**
And . . . **what are you doing here?"**

(What am I doing here?! Like it was totally normal for her to be here?!)

"I suppose **I should be asking the same,"** I said rather calmly,
all things considered.

"Well, I . . ." She peered over my shoulder. **"Breeze?"**

"Hey, **Ophelia."** Breeze approached the thoroughly bewildered
waitress. "We brought you in. **You fainted** in the street last night."

"Oh! Did I? The last thing I remember is talking to Theor, the innkeeper. He fired me the other day. He said I wasn't cut out for it, and I'm not, really. I only took the job because I'd get to hear all the rumors and earn some emeralds in the process."

"What rumors?" Breeze asked.

"Well, the people around here talk an awful lot about quests. They're like special jobs, I guess? Like this farmer I heard about: He was offering a decent stack of emeralds to anyone who could rid his farm of slimes. It took me half a day, including travel, but it was well worth it."

"Ophelia," I said. "Why are you doing this? Why are you here, in this city, hoarding emeralds?"

She bit her lip, then gestured at Breeze. "Her father sent me. The night of the party. He gave me a map, and . . ."

I glanced at Breeze, who shrugged helplessly. She seemed just as stunned as I was. Then I repeated Ophelia's words absently. "Her father . . . sent you. . . ."

"Yes," Ophelia said with a sigh. "And I really wish he hadn't. It's been so hard for me. Ever since I left, I . . ." She gave us a thoughtful look.

"He sent me on **a mission.** To **save** Villagetown. He wanted me to find an **advanced crafting table.** But **I failed** in the end. I've brought such **dishonor** to my village. . . ."

Her words hit me **like a fist. Breeze, too.**

I'm not sure how to describe what I was feeling at that exact moment. **Angry? Trolled?** But I barely had time to process what I'd heard. Seconds later, **a voice reverberated** throughout the room.

"There's a reason for all this, you know."

Near the window, the air began to **shimmer,** the transparent emptiness slowly taking on **the form of a person.**

And the person who appeared was Brio.

Breeze stormed up to him.

"Father? What does all of this mean? What have you done?"

"All will be explained." He turned to the window. "But first, I suggest you go downstairs. Breakfast is waiting, and there are some travelers who've come a long way to share it with you."

If you **don't recognize** these people, don't worry. **I didn't either at first.**

From left to right: Emerald, Lola, Stump, and Max.

"Hey, look! They're finally awake!"

"Dude! Lola! You're hogging the seat!"

"I'm gonna hurgg. I'm gonna hurgg."

"So you started my book yet?"

It seemed like **forever** since I'd last seen them.

And it was **both strange** and **comforting** to see that they looked almost nothing like villagers anymore.

37

I took a seat next to **Ophelia** and **Breeze**. "**Okay,** I can't even begin to describe **how great** it is to see you guys, **but . . .** will someone **tell me what's going on?!**"

"It's **a test,**" Stump said. "Kolb, Breeze's dad, and the mayor were **the only ones** who knew about it."

"It was **seriously confusing,**" Emerald added. "The council thought it best to **keep everything a secret,** because . . . um . . . villager logic." She **rolled her eyes.** "First, we heard that **you were in trouble.** Then Breeze **disappeared,** and suddenly **she** was in trouble. . . ."

"We wanted to see what **Ophelia, Cogboggle,** and **you** were capable of," Brio said, approaching the table. "In particular, we felt that you had to really **get out there and experience the Overworld** for yourself. If you had left knowing that it was yet **another** test, your experience wouldn't have been the same. Of course, **the forge** is something we **desperately need.** Two bats with one arrow, as the old saying goes."

He then mentioned how the mayor had started **worrying** and sent Breeze to check on me. **Cog** had been sent later to **help Ophelia.**

When I mentioned how I'd seen him earlier being chased by **three angry knights,** Brio nodded sagely. "Seems like he's forgotten all about **his duties,** then. I would like to have a word with him. I'm afraid his **pilfering** from unsuspecting travelers will not bolster the reputation of villagers. . . ."

"**Emerald's been stealing too,**" Stump said casually.

She glared at him. "**Thanks a lot, noobmaster.** I was testing out **my new ability!**"

"Looks like you need to do **a bit more testing,** then. The only thing you managed to steal from that innkeeper was **a block of wood!**"

"**Hurrmmph!** Y'know, we **do** have more important things to be discussing here, like . . . **Runt's little quest.**" She smiled at me. "**So** did you manage to find **that table thingy?**"

"I did."

I retrieved **the aeon forge** and set it on the table in front of me.

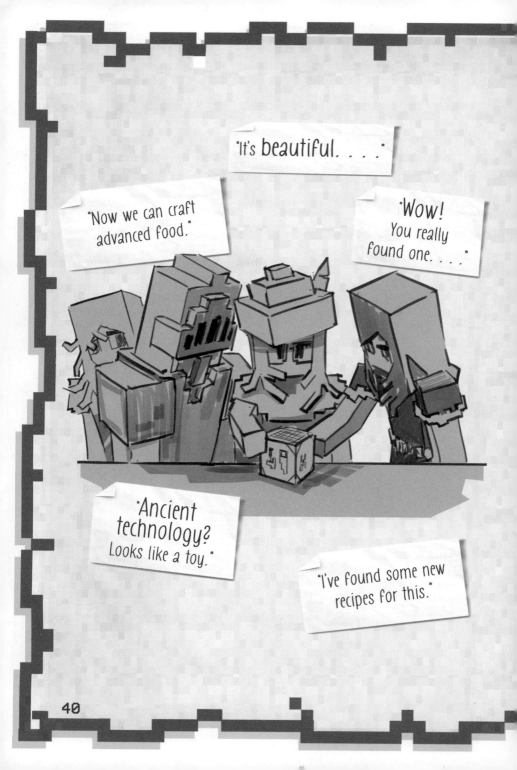

"With this," Max said, "the monsters won't **stand a chance.** Not that they've been attacking. It's been **pretty quiet** back home."

"It seems **the Eyeless One** has been focusing his efforts elsewhere for the time being," Brio said. "A great number of his minions have moved into **the eastern arm of Ravensong Forest,** to the keep known as **Stormgarden.**"

"Some pigman mentioned that," I said. "He wanted to take me there for questioning. **What is that place?**"

"It was **abandoned** by **the Knights of Aetheria** hundreds of years ago," he said. "But the monsters are now occupying the lower levels, where there aren't **too many traps.** At any rate, this means we have **some breathing room.** For now. When they return, they'll be **facing a defense** like no village has ever produced."

Once more, everyone stared down at **the forge.**

In the end, I suppose the mayor's plan **did make sense,** in that **villager** sort of way.

Now that we have this object, our village can be **seriously upgraded.** And in the process, Cog, Ophelia, and I gained **invaluable** experience.

Yet something kept **nagging at me.** "So you **send us outside,**" I said, "to see what we can do, to help us learn more about the Overworld. **Why, though?** Why was it **so important** that we learn of the outside world? I know we'll be **exploring** soon, but sending us out so far, in secret, by **ourselves** . . . it's a bit **extreme,** don't you think?"

Brio fell **silent.**

When he finally spoke, **his expression was grave.**

"I didn't want to tell you about this yet. But I suppose the council has **kept this** from you long enough." He retrieved a piece of paper from his robes. "Weeks ago, shortly before **your graduation,** a **messenger** arrived in the middle of the night. A messenger from **the** capital. **An emissary of the king.**"

He placed the paper on the table
in a **gentle way,**
as though regretful.

ROYAL NOTICE

LET IT BE KNOWN THAT—BY THE THIRD
OF DIAMONDSTAR—EVERY CITY, TOWN,
AND VILLAGE WITH NO LESS THAN ONE
HUNDRED DOORS SHALL SEND EXACTLY
FIFTEEN OF THEIR FINEST YOUNG
MEN AND WOMEN TO THE CAPITAL.
THERE THEY SHALL RECEIVE FURTHER
TRAINING AT THE GREATER AETHERIAN
ACADEMY, UPON COMPLETION OF
WHICH THEY SHALL BE CALLED UPON
BY KING RUNEHAMMER II, SEVENTH
LANTERNGUARD OF ARDENVELL.

SIGNED UPON THIS FIFTEENTH
DAY OF FROST HARVEST

For the longest moment, **overpowering silence** filled the dining hall.

Then Emerald **laughed** nervously. "**Wow,** this is, um . . . s-some kind of joke, right?"

"I don't think so," Max said. "**That's the king's seal.** The Flame of the Eternal Lantern. Only the **grand magister** knows the crafting recipe."

"**What's today?**" Stump asked. "**The twenty-third?**" He'd hardly touched the **enderpuff scone** *(enderscone for short)* in his hand, which clearly meant he was afraid. "**The third of Diamondstar** is just ten days away!"

Breeze seemed **really upset.** Her father just **sighed.** "**Aetheria City** is a long way from home," he said. "And we have no idea what **your training** may entail. Therefore, the council felt it **cruel** to send you away without **experiencing the Overworld** first." He turned to his daughter. "Breeze, **I'm sorry.** There's no other way."

"**Really?**" Stump asked. "There's **no way out** of this? We **have** to go?"

"Looks like it." Breeze **sunk** into her chair, arms crossed, and let out a deep breath before **glaring** at her father.

"Well, **I find it marvelous!**" Lola exclaimed. "Such a **delightful little surprise!** To think that we'll actually meet the **king!** Although, I **do** wonder what sort of outfit I should wear. . . ."

"If this is **what's demanded** of me," Ophelia said, herself once again, "then I'll go. And I'm sure **the members of my team** would say the same." Her **sober** expression darkened with **a hint of sadness.** "I miss them," she said, meaning her friends, the rest of **Team All-Girls.** "Why aren't they here?"

"They wanted to come," Brio said, "but felt they should **remain** in Villagetown in case of **another attack.** You've really instilled a **sense of duty** in them. **Cog's group,** on the other hand, didn't want to bother. It seems they're **not too close** to their captain."

At that exact moment, **the captain in question** decided to show up. Or perhaps I should say **thief.**

Cog looked at us, at the **forge,** at the **king's letter,** and at the mixture of sullen and cheerful expressions—well, except for Ophelia, who was **on one knee** and saying something about **the honor of the village.**

"Okay, I'm guessing I missed something." Then he **snickered.** "Oh, and I'm not talking about people's inventories."

A moment later, there were a few **shouts** in the distance.

Breeze's father gave Cog a **smoldering** look. **"Fool!** You will return what you've filched **at once!"**

"Calm down, it was **just a joke!** I only stole a ring!" He held up **an obsidian ring** and examined it. "It's a **lousy item,** anyway. Be right back, guys."

I was too stunned to say anything, but Emerald, looking **more nervous** as she read and reread the letter, asked exactly what I was thinking: **"Um,** h-how many doors does Villagetown have again?"

"375," Max said. "Wait . . . **no! 379** after the south tower."

"Oh." She blinked. **"Hey, guys,** I-I was thinking, maybe Villagetown could use a **little remodeling?** Let's be honest—all those doors are a **monster hazard,** y'know? What? Don't look at me like that! **Someone's** gotta look out for our safety!"

The conversation more or less went on like that for quite some time. What that letter said was **simply unbelievable,** and the details weren't exactly clear.

Breeze's father did mention that our training in **the capital** would be **similar** to school back home, except more advanced. Yet we had so many other questions that he simply couldn't answer. **How long** will we be there? **What is life like** in the capital? Will we ever be able to visit our parents?

As the questions dwindled, everyone turned to Max, who'd been **silent** this whole time. **To everyone's surprise,** he moved closer to the **aeon forge,** hunched over it, and carefully arranged a diagonal line of **prismarine crystals.** Suddenly, with **a brilliant green flash,** a column of **pale blue light** sprang forth from each crystal. The crystals then **merged,** forming what I could only guess was **a prismarine staff.**

As soon as this item was formed, however, **a pulsing violet light** began emanating from the forge. There was a weird, **almost sad,** noise, and the staff evaporated with a tiny puff of smoke. The violet light lingered for a moment after **this failed crafting attempt.**

"Nice job, ace.
Now how about you put that **brilliant mind** of yours to good use, stop messing with that thing, and help think of a way outta **this mess?!**"

The dining hall was not **entirely empty,** even at this early hour, and Max's **little experiment**—along with Emerald's **outburst**—had **drawn the attention** of several people. They mostly **chuckled** to themselves. That's when I noticed Breeze **wasn't there anymore. She'd disappeared without a word.**

I decided to slip away too, and I soon found her on **a balcony upstairs.** She was **alone,** arms crossed, **staring at the night sky.** . . .

"Hey."

"Hey."

"So, this training in Aetheria City," I said. "Is it really **so bad?**"

"I don't think it's going to be easy," she said. "**I really don't want to go.** Maybe it's for the best, though. My father says there are **lots of things** we still don't know about ourselves."

"Like what?"

"There are countless unseen **elements** that make up who we are, like **our level, our stats, our experience points.** But even though these elements are invisible, there is a way to see them. It's called a **visual enchantment.** All of the humans have one—**it's easy** for them to use. I'm not sure why it doesn't come **naturally** to us. We have to unlock it through **a special process.** I'm sure those **at the Academy** can show us how."

"**Hope so,**" I said. In truth, I didn't really know what she was talking about. I just wanted to **stay positive.** "**Hey** . . . back there, when your dad was talking about training in the capital, he mentioned something about **selecting a class?** What did he mean by **classes?**"

"They're like **professions,**" she said. "Only better. It's **hard** to explain. Um . . . **Urf was a Nethermancer,** right? That's a class."

She went on to tell me about some of the classes.

If someone wanted to be a **wizard,** they could gain **the Wizard class.** From there, they could move on to **more specialized spell-casting** classes like Void Mage, Nethermancer, or Monster Shepherd. Monster Shepherds sound really cool, by the way. You can summon and control beasts. You start out with animals like bats and rabbits.

"We'll gain classes in the capital, too," she said. "Once our training is complete."

"That reminds me," I said. "Sometimes, you have this troubled look. Like you know something you're not telling me."

"Oh." She retrieved a black tome from her inventory. "Just some things Kolb told me about: history again, legends, something called the Prophecy. It's all in this book. We thought it was important at first but . . . it's rather vague. Max has been trying to decipher some of its more . . . puzzling sections. Most of it was written by this Scribe named Mango who was apparently quite the eccentric person."

"I haven't even finished the book Max gave me." With a sigh, I retrieved his book from my inventory and showed her my current place.

THE UNDERWORLD

IT WAS PREVIOUSLY THOUGHT THAT THE BEDROCK LAYER WAS ONLY A SEA OF UNBREAKABLE STONE STRETCHING FOREVER DOWNWARD.

RECENTLY, HOWEVER, TUNNELS HAVE BEEN FOUND TO EXIST WITHIN BEDROCK, LEADING TO A CAVERN SYSTEM RIVALING ANY FOUND IN THE NETHER.

INDEED, BELOW OUR OVERWORLD EXISTS ANOTHER WORLD, WHICH OVERWORLDIAN SAGES HAVE COINED THE UNDERWORLD.

MOOSHROOMS ARE NATIVE TO THIS REALM; ALSO COMMONPLACE ARE VAST LAKES OF WATER, LAVA, AND EVEN FORESTS OF GIANT MUSHROOMS.

OF COURSE, THERE ARE ORES THAT CAN ONLY BE FOUND IN THESE DEPTHS. BUT THEY ARE MUCH HARDER TO MINE, BEING ENCASED IN BEDROCK.

"So. **Anything else you've been hiding from me?**" I asked, closing the book.

"**Nope.** Well, there **is** one more thing . . . but **it's a surprise.**"

"I see. **Do** go on."

She **smiled.** "It wouldn't be **a surprise** if I just told you here, now would it? You'll see when we **get back home.**"

"**Okay.** Hey, **listen.** I know you're sad that we have to go, but maybe it won't be **so bad?** I read a lot of books too, you know, and **the capital really sounds amazing.**"

"I know. It's just . . . I'm not much of a **city girl.** I like farming, remember?"

"I remember," I said. "And someday, I'll help you **build that farm.**"

"**Promise?**"

Oh no, I thought. *Should I make **this** promise? I'm not the best at building. Truth be told, I came dangerously close to making one of those **building fails.** Oh well. After yesterday, I'm pretty sure I can handle just about anything. So long as **she's** with me . . .*

"Prom—"

The doors behind us **swung open.**

The person who'd opened them was **a villager.** But it was hard to tell. In fact, looking at him, it was **impossible to believe** that he had ever seen a place filled with farms and chickens and sheep. Upon his **silver breastplate** was a sigil identical to **the king's seal,** and he was holding a lantern that gave off a cozy glow. He also had **bluish-gray hair.** Clearly, he no longer followed villager **tradition.**

He joined us at the fence rail **where we were stargazing.**

"**You must be Breeze.** It's **a pleasure** to meet you." He **bowed gracefully.** His accent, though unusual, was just as graceful. "I have been **wanting to speak with you** for quite some time."

Breeze gave him a **strange** look.

"And you are?"

"Ah! Yes." He bowed again. "**Please forgive me,** my lady. I have been riding for two days. I am Sir **Elric Darkbane, Knight of Aetheria,** and I have come to ensure your **safe passage** to the capital. I'm afraid you must prepare **without delay,** for we will leave shortly."

I'd stopped listening at Sir Elric. *It's him?! Like, really?!* The guy standing before us was **famous** throughout Ardenvell, a **legendary** knight widely considered to be **the best swordsman in the entire world.** *(I actually have a painting of him in my bedroom. Well, okay, apparently it doesn't look a lot like him.)*

Then I remembered that **the Knights of Aetheria** always carry **lanterns** like that during ceremonies or when meeting **honored** guests. It's just something they do. **A tradition.** For them, the lantern symbolizes light, peace, the melting away of darkness. Even **the king** himself carries one—at all times, no less—though his lantern is unique: **a legendary-tier item** with **eight** different enchantments.

"We will pass **very close** to your home village," he continued, "so **saying goodbye to your loved ones** will not be an inconvenience. Of course, I want to say that I cannot imagine what you must be feeling right now, but I once lived in **Moonglow.** The **very first village** to fall. The one thing I can say with certainty is that, although you will learn **new customs** and an entirely **different way** of life, you will always be a villager at heart. Even as the past fades away, **who you truly are** will never change. And dare I say that you will easily grow accustomed to your new life, as you are one who looks not to the past, or even the present, but **the future.** Face the problems you have not yet had."

That last phrase caught me by surprise. Kolb had said those **exact same words** a few times before. Breeze looked **shocked** as well. "What? How do you know that?"

He smiled. "Was this not **a common saying** in your home village of **Shadowbrook?** I know much about you. It could be said that you are rather **famous** **in the West.** I hope I'm not too **brazen** in asking if what they say is true? **The imprisonment? The experiments?"**

"Yes, **it's true,** but . . ."

"Stories travel far, my lady, and there is **no tale more inspiring** than yours. The girl who escaped **the Eyeless One,** tormented and forever changed, only to rise back up and **fight again.** That is why, in the West, you have many **supporters.** I am among them."

I gave Breeze a look that said: *"On any other day, this would have been a huge surprise. But after yesterday? Nope. Nothing really fazes me anymore."*

Another knight walked through the doorway and saluted **Elric.** "Sir, I bring **excellent** news. **Etherly Keep** has been reclaimed, and the remaining undead have been **destroyed.** Furthermore, Herobrine's forces have been **driven from Dawnsbloom** entirely. As unbelievable as it may seem, **we are already winning** this war!"

"**So it appears.** Perhaps **Lady Luck** is finally on our side. What of the **initiates?**"

"The rest have just arrived," the knight said. "We are **ready to leave** at a moment's notice."

"Then I guess **it's time.**" Elric smiled at us and bowed once more. "I will go check on **the others.** See you outside?"

After the knights left, I turned to Breeze. "**So what were you saying earlier?** Something about how you didn't want to go? **Huh.**" I shrugged. "The capital doesn't sound **so bad** to me."

"You're still **helping me build that farm** when we get back," she said with a wink. "Don't think I didn't hear you **promise.**"

She took me by the hand again and pulled me back inside. Many knights stood at attention in the hall, a row on each side. The combined glow of their lanterns was **overwhelming:** As we walked past, it seemed as though we'd stepped not into **the hall of an inn** but **a tunnel of brilliant, wavering light.**

It was **still dark** when we gathered outside.

Although it was **hard to tell** without looking up to the sky. **Those lanterns** were everywhere, bathing the streets in a **golden glow,** as well as the knights who held them.

As might be expected, even at this hour, **a lot** of townsfolk were lingering around. They whispered and **giggled,** pointing here and there. Not only at the knights, of course, but also at us: **the nine heroic villagers** who would soon be traveling to **Aetheria City.**

While the onlookers gathered, a rotund man in fancy-looking clothes **rolled** in our direction. Well, he wasn't on wheels or anything—it was just how he walked.

With a wavelike motion of his arm, he shouted at the townsfolk:

"**Sound the horns, you peasants!** It is a marvelous occasion we witness! **These fine villagers** are going to train in the capital!"

Suddenly, a group of townsfolk with horn-like musical instruments rushed out from the crowd and immediately started playing. I've **never heard** music like it before, and I hope to never hear it again. The deep and rumbling sounds they made were **hideous,** like some giant, **flatulent** cow.

The man **facepalmed.** It seemed things were not going according to plan. Then he waved downward, as if **signaling** them to stop. The horns quieted. Well, not all at once—a few stragglers trailed off **pitifully.**

·Disgraceful! Have you not practiced?! You **bring shame** to us all!"

Then this **fancifully dressed** man *(maybe the mayor of Owl's Reach?)* turned to the **Aetherian Knights,** approaching their leader. ·**Sir Elric Darkbane.**" He bowed deeply. "It is a pleasure as always. Please forgive them. Not playing **their best,** I'm afraid. It seems they've had a bit too much **stormberry ale** in light of our little celebration. And then, being so far from Aetheria City, surely you can imagine **we don't often play** the capital's anthem."

"**It is nothing,**" Elric said. "These **customs** have never concerned me much. And perhaps I have even grown weary of such music over time. It's played endlessly at **the Academy,** even on the smallest of occasions."

The mayor *(so it was him)* bowed once more. "And with regret, I must say that **our own initiates** already left three days ago. They were **so excited. . . . Oh yes,** so very excited, indeed, to see such a glorious city, and further, I must add that . . ."

He spoke like this for **some time.** No way am I writing all that down. At last, upon wishing us farewell, the mayor left us in peace.

Sir Elric then walked past each villager present, **nodding with respect.** He stopped at **Emerald,** who was sitting on the front steps of the inn, **half-asleep,** elbow on knee, hand propping up one side of her face. Finally, he glanced **at me.**

"Your friends say **you do not have a horse,**" he said quizzically.

"As **crazy** as it sounds," I said, "**you can blame a Nethermancer** named Urf for that."

"Very well." He turned to another knight. "**Zigurd.** The villager Runt no longer has a horse. Would you be so kind as to **find one for him?**"

With a scowl so **intense** it was almost comical, Zigurd looked at the other knights as though he couldn't believe what he'd just heard. Then he **glared** at the musicians, who were still holding their horns, then at me, and shook his head in **disgust.**

"This is **noobery,**" he muttered. "Utter **noobery.**"

"**Ye,** it is," another knight said. "How will that lad make it through training if he can't keep track of his own horse?"

"Ye. Almost makes you wonder if—"

"**Enough!**" Elric snapped. "Zigurd. You are a **Knight of Aetheria,** and you will begin **acting** like one, instead of grumbling like a zombie pigman. **Is that understood?**"

". . . Ye, **I'm on it,**" Zigurd said. Still grumbling, he took off to the stables. "I just want to go **home.** . . ."

Elric looked at us once more. "We should replenish **our food bars** before setting out." He raised a hand. A hotbar appeared before him.

"Anyone care for a stormberry roll?"

To a villager, these screens are always **a strange sight.** We can only see our own inventories. It's simply **impossible** to conjure these windows into view for others. The Legionnaires can, of course, but they don't belong to **this reality.** This kind of magic comes **naturally** to them.

Elric, however, was a villager, **born of this world.** An **NPC**—not a so-called **player. It shouldn't have been possible** for him.

"That's part of your **visual enchantment,**" I said. "Isn't it? How did you **unlock it?**"

"I underwent **special training,**" he said. "In **the Tower Eternal.** Once you begin your studies, **the magisters** there will assist you in his regard."

"How does it work, anyway?" Stump asked. "It's like . . . **magic?**"

"Ye. At least, that is what many believe. But **no one knows** how we came to possess such enchantment. Some say it exists **deep inside us,** infused within our blood long ago. Back when magic was still **commonplace.**" Elric grinned. "Of course, those are the same people who think there are **biomes on the moon.**"

"On the **moon?**" Stump looked up into the cold black sky with an expression of confusion mixed with happiness—as though someone had told him that creepers **were actually vegetables. 'Whoaaaa . . .'**

Elric turned to another knight, who was, perhaps, the youngest among the nine knights present. "**Konrad!** Have the horses completely **recovered?**"

"They have, sir!" Konrad saluted. "Full endurance bars across the board!"

"Excellent. And the Swiftness potions?"

"Not too many left, I'm afraid. Just under five saddle chests."

"No matter. That will do." Elric flashed a weary smile. "All right, everyone. We leave soon. There is another inn to the south, the Inn of the Laughing Cow, where we will rest for the night. In the morning, we will ride through Ravensong Forest and hit the moon elf village of Glimfrost. Since their village is so close to Stormgarden, we would like to check on them. And, by tomorrow's eve, we will arrive at your home." He turned back to the young knight. "Oh, Konrad! Make sure each villager has adequate supplies: Healing Ills, stormberry rolls. These initiates are important. We take no chances today."

Konrad saluted. "At once, sir!"

Emerald—still half asleep—suddenly stirred. "Huh? Boats?"

Stump nudged me. "Hey," he whispered. "What does 'noobery' mean?"

We were off before sunrise.

At first, I didn't believe we could reach Villagetown in less than two days. But as we blazed our way south, the horses were continuously provided with **potions of Swiftness VII**—extended duration. The countless plains biomes **flew by.**

Max figured we were traveling at least **twice the speed** of a mine cart on **powered rails.** To me, it felt like we were going even faster than that. Take a creeper, a slimeball, and a kitten. Attach said kitten to the creeper's behind using the slimeball. Watch as the creeper zooms off super fast.

That's <u>how fast</u> we were traveling.

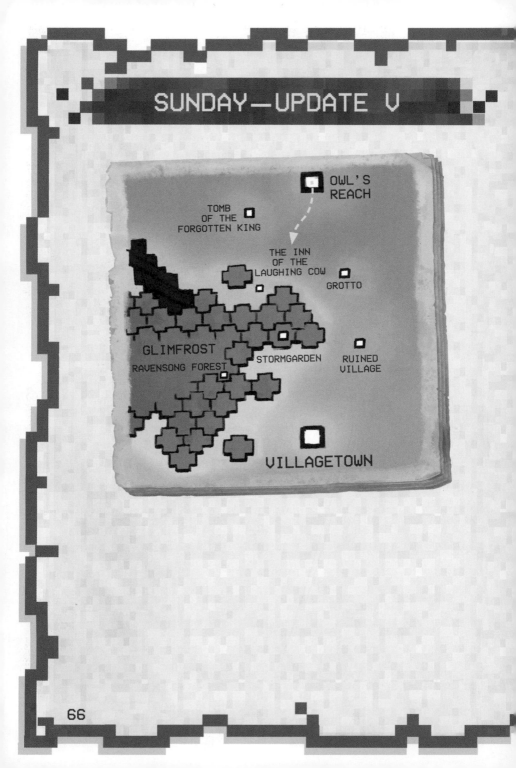

SUNDAY—UPDATE VI

We rode through plains,

We rode through savanna,

We rode through hills and streams,

At times, we rode swiftly,

At times, we rode carefully,

More than a noob ever dreams.

Do you like it?

It's a little poem I wrote called "**We Traveled through the Overworld for Hours and Hours, and It Was Really, Really Boring.**"

SUNDAY—UPDATE VII

OWL'S REACH

TOMB OF THE FORGOTTEN KING

THE INN OF THE LAUGHING COW

GROTTO

GLIMFROST

RAVENSONG FOREST

STORMGARDEN

RUINED VILLAGE

VILLAGETOWN

The Inn of the Laughing Cow

We finally came across **something besides grass.**

It was **a massive** structure—looking a bit lonely on the savanna—at least **three times the size of the Enchanted Dragon,** though the design was mostly the same. And the same kind of people occupied it: Imagine a person, **any type of person,** from pirate to fortune-teller. Anyone who came to mind could be found inside.

Needless to say, the entrance of **nine villagers** and **ten knights** drew **little attention.** Well, except for the attention of some waitress in the same outfit Ophelia still had on. She showed us this piece of paper that had a bunch of different **food items** on it.

I ordered an **enchanted moonseed muffin.** It had **little sparkle effects.** Imported straight from the capital, she said.

Let me tell you, that muffin was **perfect.** Whoever crafted it definitely had a Crafting skill that was at least fifty points higher than mine; the one time I tried crafting muffins, not only did I burn them but also the **furnace** caught on fire. I took another bite. *Hmm. At least 150 Crafting skill.* Another bite. *Possibly even 175.*

Stump ordered the same thing I did. After his first bite, he said a single word: "**Dude.**" The second bite was followed by the same word, only with a little bit more excitement: "**Dude.**" Each bite thereafter was another "**dude**" of ever **increasing pitch, volume, excitement,** and/ or **confusion.** Once, he even spoke in a different accent.

"Dude."

"DUDE . . . ?!"

". . . DEHWD."

"Dude."

"DUDE!!!"

After finishing mine, I left the table and stepped outside. The inn's noise had been **getting to me,** which I found **a bit odd.** Noise had never really bothered me before. Villagetown was often **pure chaos:** all the hammering of blacksmiths and bleating of sheep, the **angry shouting** of some trade gone wrong. . . .

Maybe I was growing accustomed to the **silence of the Overworld.**

"Hey."

A familiar voice to my right. **No surprise.**

"Hey." I glanced sidelong in her direction. "**Emerald** said the rooms we'll be staying in are **out of this world.** In the capital, I mean. From the way she spoke, it sounded like even **bedroom slippers** are **enchanted.** And the bathroom cauldrons are **made of gold.**"

71

She smiled at **my lame** attempt at humor. **Slightly.** "You should be **more serious.** We have a lot to think about."

"Does this look like the face of a joking man? We'll be living **like kings,** she says." At last, **I smiled too.** "Oh, I suppose there's no need to cheer you up, is there? You're **Breeze,** she who escaped from the clutches of **the Eyeless One.** It must be **exciting** to know you're going to a place filled with so many **adoring fans.**"

"I still have a hard time believing it," she said. "How do so many people even know about . . . **that.**"

That.

By "that," she meant **her past.**

It definitely is a **curious** story. But even now, I know few details. She's never spoken about being **captured** and **experimented** upon, and I've always found it rude to ask. I've heard **rumors,** sure. Rumors I won't write here. I'd never do that without **her permission.**

As her smile **faded,** my mind raced to think of a good way to change the subject. **Luckily,** the inn's front door creaked open, saving me the effort.

An **old man** in threadbare brown robes hobbled outside. The robe had many dark red patches, the largest of which had white stitching that resembled **the face of a smiling kitten.** Another patch looked like **a green bird.** Both this person and his robes seemed **worn and faded.** If someone had told me that this ancient man lived in an item chest along with five rabbits and two cats, I **totally** would have believed it. Strangely, he displayed **no emotion. None whatsoever.** As I said, that inn held **any** type of person you could **imagine.**

The man **slowly hobbled** up to us.

The whole time he did, **he never took his eyes off Breeze.**

I leaned over to her and said in a low voice, "Seems you have admirers **even here.**"

The elderly man continued to stare at her as he crept forward. There was **something off** about him, I felt. Well, okay, an old man with a kitten and a bird on his robes definitely **isn't** normal, but . . . it was more than that. It was **the complete lack of emotion.** The shambling gait. I was getting some **really creepy** vibes.

Still looking at Breeze, he stopped just outside of sword distance, opened his mouth, and whispered in a **peculiarly hollow** tone:

"Alyss . . ."

An odd-sounding name: **uh-LYSS.**

Breeze looked **shaken.** "Runt. **Get back.**"

Something in her voice—and in the man himself—gave me **the total chills.**

My instincts told me that the figure before us was not some **harmless** old man. Not any kind of person at all.

Suddenly, the **"man"** surged forward. Arms outstretched. **Reaching. Grasping.** Clawing. Movements I'd seen so many times before.

Yet he never reached her. **My swords** reached him first. In less than a second, both **diamond** and **obsidian** were flying at him, removing his health in an instant. Breeze had always been **quick on her feet,** but at this point she hadn't yet drawn her blades. I guess I was **on top of my game** today. What was **in** those muffins?!

With a **low moan,** what appeared to be the elderly man sank to the ground. I don't even know how to describe what happened next, but I'll try. The man's outward appearance was actually **some kind of trick,** like **a magical costume,** that dissolved into **wisps of shadow.** What remained was a **shadowy** figure. It crumbled into **black shreds,** which then also dissolved—leaving behind only a pile of glimmering blue-white dust.

Eerie silence followed.

". . . Breeze."

"Yeah."

"What was that?"

"Don't know."

"I've never heard of **shape-shifting zombies.**"

She shook her head. "No, I think it was more like . . . **an illusion.**"

Illusion, huh . . .

I recalled noticing the **"old man"** in the inn, a while earlier. He was standing by the entrance. Just standing there. I'd never suspected a thing. It wasn't until I really looked closely that I sensed **something was off** about him. The disguise, or illusion, had been quite **convincing.**

Whatever that thing was, it'd been searching for Breeze—and **only** Breeze.

Not once had it looked at me.

Why?

And why did it call her

<u>a completely different name . . . ?</u>

Or had I misheard? Had it **really** whispered a name? Or had it simply made the kind of sound the undead normally make? **A hiss,** maybe? Or perhaps it had been speaking in **an unknown tongue,** and whispering the word **"alyss"** was just **some kind of threat** or curse. As would naturally be expected of a shadowy zombie/ghost.

"I thought I heard it **whisper** something," I said. "It was so quiet, but it . . . it almost sounded like a name. **Alyss.**"

"I . . . **didn't hear anything,**" she said. "Maybe it was **the wind.**"

"**Huh. Yeah.** Maybe it was."

But there wasn't any wind.

The grass was as **still** as a painting.

Whatever. Maybe it said something; maybe it didn't. I was **too tired** for this.

The front door of the inn **creaked** open again. A group of robed humans emerged, heading for the stables. **Breeze's father** appeared behind them. Upon seeing our drawn weapons and the pile of **shimmering dust,** he rushed over, face filled with **alarm.**

"You must **be more careful,**" he said. "Despite his name, **the Eyeless One** has many eyes, and they are everywhere." Crouching down, he scooped up a handful of the brilliant white dust. It sifted through his fingers like sand. "**Ethereal Essence.** There are several forms of undead that leave this residue when slain. But almost never in **such great quantity.** Tell me, what did it look like? Was it **incorporeal?**"

I blinked. "**Incorporeal?**"

"**Spectral.** Ghostlike. A transparent or shadowy form."

"Its true form resembled **a husk made of shadow,**" Breeze said. "Yet, until the moment it fell, it appeared to be an . . ."

As she shared the story, her father nodded sagely.

"I've heard of undead beings that can appear as any of their past victims. In addition, they can **inflict hideous maladies** with only a single touch. They use their illusion to get close to you. By then, it's often too late." He stood. "Consider yourselves **lucky.** And, from now on, don't go wandering off like that." It seemed like he was only speaking to his daughter when he added: "**Nowhere will you be safe.** Not here, not in Villagetown, not even in the heart of the capital. No matter where you are, you must never lower your guard."

"I'm **sorry,**" she said. "I'll be more careful."

"Let's go back inside," he said. "I fear we're being watched even now."

When he said this, I noticed someone **over his shoulder,** in the distance. I couldn't make him out clearly. It was getting late, the sun falling red over golden-orange savanna. Even so, I could see that it was some **peasant-like person** in simple earth-tone clothes.

Arms at his sides, he was **staring** at us in much the same way as the creature from earlier. He **slowly** approached. On his belt were **three pouches,** looking like miniature item chests. A **traveling merchant,** then. That was what it **wanted** us to think. Indeed, like the other being, the disguise was rather convincing. Even so, I could see that there was no intelligence in those **dull brown eyes.** I watched this "**humble trader**" creep forward with the mindless, relentless determination of **a zombie.** When it stopped within sword distance, I reached up behind me, resting my right hand upon the pommel of my diamond weapon.

The man **opened** his mouth. **Closed it.**

Just try it, I thought. *Go on. Extend your arms.*

He opened his mouth again: "Milord? Care for **a stormberry roll?**"

". . ."

I **lowered** my arm.

"**Come,**" Brio said. "You two must be exhausted. Let's get you to your rooms."

Breeze pointed at the pile of dust with a boot. "Should we . . . **take that?**"

"I suppose we should," her father said. "It's used in **several advanced recipes.** Mainly for accessories. **One type of amulet,** if I recall."

He should have just said **free cool stuff.** I instantly fell to my knees, gathering as much as I could.

Breeze did the same, though **reluctantly.** "Never thought zombie dust could be **valuable.**"

The merchant gave us the **strangest** look when she said that. . . .

When we went back inside, I paid much more attention to the random people at the tables. **A dark dwarf** in fanciful gold armor, laughing. No, he wasn't one of them. **A human** in basic leather, making a weird face as he took a sip of some potion. No, **he's okay.** A villager wearing a full set of iron armor, with a helmet almost covering his eyes.

Hmm, he looks a little suspicious, doesn't he? He's just sitting there staring ahead, no emotion. Now he's slowly turning his head in my direction. Oh, now he's staring at me, still no emotion. Could it be? Is it another mysterious shape-shifting zombie entity?!

The villager wiped away some sparkling crumbs. ". . . Dude. Those muffins? **Amazing,** with like five Zs."

It was just Stump.

"By the way," he said, "I got us a room. Don't worry. **I won't snore.**"

The knights were already bidding everyone goodnight or heading to their rooms, as were Breeze and her father, Max, Lola, and Ophelia.

Emerald was at another table, chatting with some guy. He appeared to be **an elf of some kind,** with long ears, longer hair, and a feathered cap just like mine. Only his cap was red and didn't have any mold on it. He also had a **stringed musical instrument** on the table in front of him.

I yawned. Riding at full speed for an entire day is **super tiring.** I went straight to my room and crashed onto my bed, where I am right now. Despite my exhaustion, I haven't been able to sleep. That zombie from earlier was **just too much.** Or ghost. **Or whatever it was.**

Alyss . . .

What does it mean?!

Hmm. You know, Max has **a dictionary.** Seeing how he **is** my **personal library,** I'm going drag him here right now.

Correction. Max has **five** dictionaries: *Common*, *Ancient*, *Old Aetherian*, *Enderscript*, and *Netherian*.

Strangely, the word **"alyss"** does not appear to exist in any of these languages. Furthermore, the entity I saw isn't listed in **either** of the two books Max has relating to the undead.

"Whatever you encountered," Max said, "I'm guessing it's almost **never** seen in the Overworld. At any rate, the presence of something like that is **worrying.** It means a lot of things. Of course, **none of them** are **good.**"

"What about that word?"

"Are you sure that's what it said? **'Alyss'?**"

"Could have been a **moan** or something. It **was** a type of zombie, after all. Who knows? Breeze said she didn't hear it, so . . ."

I glanced at the other books piled on the table. The former librarian devoted **at least half** of his inventory space to books. I read some of the many titles.

On Zombies: Monster Hunter's Compendium

From Crypt Slimes to Nightshades: Encyclopedia of Undead

History of Aetheria: Volumes I & II

Coves, Shrines, & Lighthouses: Secret and Forgotten Locales

How to Properly Smelt an Iron Slime

The Divine Weapons

Urg the Barbarian

Moon Elves & Dusk Elves

The Netherian Road: A Traveler's Guide

Calling Your First Familiar

Tome of Wizardry: A Guide to Basic Spells

After **browsing** through this miniature library, I finally spoke up. "So, Max . . . Breeze has been hiding things. Things related to something called **the Prophecy.** Care to **fill me in?** What have I **missed** since I left?"

"Best thing you could do would be to read that book she gave you. I know you don't like reading, **but . . ."**

I **gasped.** "You know I love books **nearly** as much as you. I proudly boast of having **thousands of pages** under my belt. With just a few thousand more, dare I say my knowledge of the world would rival the **Grand Magister's.**" I looked around before adding: "Whoever he is."

Max **sighed.** "Then why is it you always treat me like your personal library?"

I gasped **again.** "Personal library? I've never thought of you as anything other than **one of my closest** friends. A friend who . . . just so **happens** to have a very large number of books at his disposal. Oh fine. **You're right.** But aren't you the one always asking me to **help you research?** Aren't you the one who gives me so many books to read?"

"Yeah. **Sorry.** Hey, I don't mind helping out. I've just been kind of busy these days."

"Busy **with what?**"

He ignored my question and asked one himself: "Have you thought about what class you want to become? **Any idea?**"

"I've given it some thought, but Breeze said there are **over one hundred** different classes. I'd like to at least see **a list** before I make any real decisions. What if I decided to become a **Knight,** only to find out there's a **Swashbuckler** class?" I glanced at the *Tome of Wizardry.* "How about you? I take it you want to become **a magician** of some type?"

"I do," he said. "Not sure what, though. Probably start off as a basic Wizard."

The door creaked open. *(Always with the doors creaking open.)*

It was **Emerald.** She peeked in. "What are **you nerds** doing?"

"Nothing your simple mind could fathom," Max said. "**Away with ye, foul noobling.**"

With a *hurrmph*, she pushed the door open and stepped inside. She was holding **the stringed instrument** that was on the table earlier. She held it up. "Look what I **traded** for."

SILVER LYRE
INSTRUMENT
+5 MUSIC SKILL

"**Why would you trade for that?**" I asked. "Did those guys with the horns not discourage you from ever wanting to play a musical instrument?"

"Nope. In fact, ever since I learned about classes, I've been flirting with the idea of **becoming a Bard.** And you know that guy downstairs with the red hat? He just happens to be one. **His name's Flynn.**

I asked him **a million questions** about his class, and I have to say, being a Bard sounds **really fun.** So it's **official.** I've decided. Once we begin our training, that's what I'm going to be."

I glanced at her. Then at **the lyre.** Then at her again. "And . . . **what does a Bard do,** exactly?"

"**Um . . .** they can play songs with **magical effects.** There's one song that can **heal.** Another song that can **put monsters to sleep.** They're abilities, of course, which I'll need to learn. Oh, they're also kinda **adept** in the shadier skills. For example, you need to have at least some knowledge of **thieving skills** to become a Bard. As well as a decent Music skill, **obviously.**"

As she strummed her lyre, Max winced in **agony.** "On that note," he said, "I'd best be off." He started gathering all his books. "Should be **studying up on spells,** anyway." Before he left, he added: "Make sure to read up on **the Prophecy.**"

"Will do."

"You don't want to do that," Emerald said. "It's **way** too confusing."

"Perhaps you could give me a brief rundown, then. After all, you're quite **close with Kolb.**"

"Sure."

She set her lyre down on the table
and sat across from me.
Little did I know
just what she was going to reveal. . . .

"It's like this," Emerald said. "The Prophecy is **more** than just a prophecy. It involves a **quest,** a **massive, extremely** complicated one. It could take years to finish. Once it's completed, winning the war will be **infinitely easier.** Otherwise, peace will be **impossible.** *For darkness will spread across the land.*" She said that last part in a **deep voice,** trying to sound heroic. **Then she smiled** and added in her normal voice: "With me so far?"

I **squinted** at her. "I'm not five."

"**Okay.** Well, some people are **vital** to this quest. There are hundreds of them all across the world—from knights to shopkeepers, dwarves to villagers. Despite their various backgrounds, these people all have **one thing in common.** *They're the descendants of heroes who fought in the Second Great War.* These people are **special.** They're able to do things most people cannot. **It's in their blood.** What's more, some of these people possess **relics** or key information that has been passed down through their family lines." She paused. "Still with me?"

"**I think.** But how is this quest supposedly completed?"

"No one really knows. All the books we have on **the Prophecy** are incomplete. Some are missing a lot of pages, even entire chapters. We do know it involves restoring **a bunch of old weapons.**"

"Old weapons? **No.** You can't be talking about the ones from **that fairy tale. . . .**"

She nodded.

"You mean they're **real?**"

"Yes."

"Real as in, you can touch them? Like with your hands?"

"Dude." She gave me **an exhausted look. "I've seen one myself.**"

". . ."

This is the sound I make when I'm in **total shock.**

Emerald Shadowcroft had just dealt **a critical hit** to my simple mind.

What she said next was a **powerful** follow-up strike. Like the second half of a fatal combo that left me totally stunned.

"**Kolb has one,**" she said. "He's had it ever since he arrived in this world. He just didn't tell us. **He's been hiding it** this whole time." She sighed. "I know, right?"

"So **he's some kind of hero,** then?"

Emerald nodded. "Something like that. But he's not a lone hero who will **magically** save the day; there's a lot more to this than just a single person. And honestly, that sword he has is pretty much worthless. **It's broken,** and restoring it will take forever. **Seven other pieces** are scattered across the Overworld."

I sighed. "Well, you were right. This is **a lot** to take in."

"**There's more,**" she said. "Wanna know why he came to Villagetown? Some guy sent him here on **a quest.** He didn't know why, at first. Only recently did he learn he was meant to find you. And Breeze. Pebble, too. **You are all descendants**—you're all linked to that quest. So it's no **coincidence** that you became friends. **You were meant to.** Call it destiny, if you want. **The will of the gods.** Or call it part of the game's code. Whatever it is, **mysterious forces** are at work."

"But why? Why are **we** important?"

"Like I said, we need to learn more in the capital. Guess it's **no coincidence** that we're being sent there, right? There's only one thing I know for sure. You are **bound by blood** to these events. If we think of this world as a game, you'd be called **Quest NPCs.** A step above ordinary NPCs. And it sounds like you have **a bigger role** to play than most."

90

". . ."

Quest NPCs . . .

So I'm linked by blood to some **major event.**

Like Emerald said, if you're **a Believer,** you call it destiny.

Otherwise, you think of it as the laws of a game, countless lines of

code. Whatever you choose to believe, in the end, isn't that important.

It's as though we're all **tiny gears** in some massive redstone machine.

I heard the lightest footsteps behind me.

"I wanted to tell you," Breeze said. "It's just that . . . you already had

so much going on. I didn't want you **to feel overwhelmed. . . ."**

"It's fine," I said. **"Thank you."**

Honestly, I was **glad** she didn't tell me.

Emerald and I have always been **on the same level.** She explained

it in a way I could **easily** understand.

The future Bard rose from her seat. "Sorry, Breeze. Didn't mean

to **steal a moment** from you. Just thought Runt should know.

Y'know?"

"Doesn't matter," Breeze said. "I didn't know where to begin

anyway. I've never talked with the Legionnaires much."

Emerald grabbed **her lyre.** "All right, guys, I'm out. Gonna try practicing some more. And Runt, try not to think about it so much. You're **destined** to assist the Overworld in some way, but so are plenty of other people. From shopkeepers to hermits living in mountain caves. You're far from being **the only** descendant. And then, even if you **weren't** destined to help out . . . you would anyway, **right?**" She **winked.** "Night, guys."

After Emerald left, Breeze gave me **a worried look.** "You okay?"

"Yeah. It's a lot to **process,** but . . ."

"When they first read **the Prophecy,** they thought you were one of the only ones tied into this. But as they read more, they learned that there are **hundreds.** But that's all we know for now. We'll find out more in **Aetheria City,** I think. In the **Tower Eternal.**" She suddenly seemed wiped out. "Gonna lie down. **Exhausted.** Night."

"**Hey.**"

". . . ?"

"Is this why **that thing** was after you? Are we being . . . **hunted?**"

She nodded. "If we really are so important in this story, it's in **the Eyeless One's** best interests to . . . **cross us out.**"

I felt **a chill** when she said this, and I remembered how she'd reacted to the old man—how **afraid** she'd sounded. And I recalled what her father had told her: "Nowhere will you be safe. . . ."

"**Wait,** this isn't the first time something has attacked you like that," I said. "It's happened **before,** hasn't it? Maybe it wasn't a zombie disguised as an old man, or a ghost, whatever it was, but . . . **other things** have come for **you** in the past, haven't they?"

". . ."

"Well?"

She sighed. "I won't lie to you. **It's true.** After we escaped from our imprisonment, **the Eyeless One** sent his servants after us. They were much different from what we saw today, but . . . always **something terrible.**"

"But nothing seemed to be looking for you in Villagetown."

"We figured out a way to **evade them** before we found your village."

"How?"

"That's . . . a story for **another day.** I don't want to think about it right now."

She looked away with the same **troubled** expression she often had. Today, I finally knew why. **Forever hunted . . .**

"Night."

After she left, I stood there like an iron golem, thinking over and over about what I'd just learned. If everything I heard tonight is true, **dark times** are ahead. For me. For her. Our shoulders bear **the weight** of not only a village but also the **entire world.**

I had all kinds of **nightmares** tonight. And when I woke up from them, I couldn't stop thinking about this **mysterious Prophecy** . . . and what my involvement meant.

Stump was in his bed now, lightly **snoring.** He must have come back to the room after I fell asleep. I still **felt paranoid** after all those dreams, and I went to the window. It was morning, technically, but it was still dark. I didn't see **anyone** outside. I checked the hallway, too. Just to be sure. Then I went back to my bed and sat down to think.

You are bound by blood to these events. . . .

What Emerald had told me was **crazy enough,** but when Breeze confirmed that we're now being stalked by creepy undead things, it really was like an **ultimate combo attack** that slammed me into the ground so hard I bounced then bounced again. Do those girls have no mercy? **None?** They could have at least ordered some tea before telling me all that, right? A nice warm cup of **cocoa-bean tea?** Served in a mug with powdered sugar on top? I saw that on the menu.

With a sigh, I glanced at my snoring friend. He had a book in his hands.

STUMP'S JOURNAL
SUNDAY—UPDATE II

JUST TRADED FOR A NEW SHIELD IN THE MAIN HALL. THE GUY WOULDN'T BUDGE ON THE PRICE. SO FRUSTRATING. I DON'T HAVE A SINGLE EMERALD LEFT. OH WELL. IT'S WORTH IT. I KNOW OUR QUEST WILL BE HARD. I ONLY HOPE I CAN PROTECT MY FRIENDS. THEY'RE EVERYTHING TO ME. . . .

I placed his diary back in his hands.

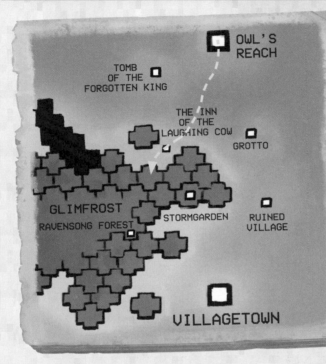

"We quickly ate our breakfast,
And rode to the southwest,
To a dark and creepy forest,
Which Lola mapped her best,
To the south we'll see the moon elves,
In their woods we'll stop to rest,
While there we must act proper,
For Stump it's quite a test."

97

No, **that's not a poem.** Nor is it mine.

It's a song Emerald sang as we entered northern **Ravensong.**

I can only hope her **singing** is tied to her Music skill, and that her

Music skill goes up **very, very fast** once we get to the Academy. . . .

Northern
Ravensong Forest

A bat with glowing
red eyes watching us . . .

Notice the ruins of
ancient fortresses.
They fell during the
Second Great War.

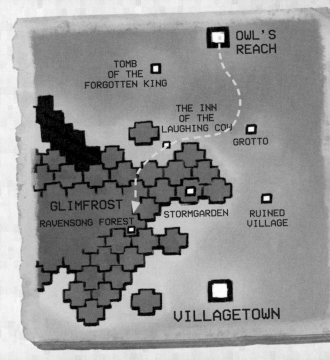

OWL'S REACH

TOMB OF THE FORGOTTEN KING

THE INN OF THE LAUGHING COW

GROTTO

GLIMFROST

RAVENSONG FOREST

STORMGARDEN

RUINED VILLAGE

VILLAGETOWN

"We reached the woods before noon,
I thought we'd reached the moon. . . ."

Before long, the tall pines gave way to an **unbelievable** sight.

Upon first seeing **the silverwood,** it really did seem as though we were on **the moon.**

While my thoughts had been dwelling on the ominous Prophecy and on being hunted forever by beings of the night, all of that was **instantly swept away.**

Among a sea of silvery grass stood bushes with **violet leaves,** gossamer white flowers, red and blue spruce, and trees so large they would have even dwarfed **dark oaks.** Far above stretched a canopy almost **the color of ice.** Glowing pools dotted the landscape here and there. Only when I saw these woods did I really understand how **amazing** our world **really** is, how vast and diverse, filled with places that darkness can never reach.

When we stopped to feed the horses more **Swiftness** potions, Breeze pointed to what appeared to be a block of green glowstone suspended from the leaves. "That's **a moonstone lantern.** Only **the moon elves** know how to craft them. Their light is **said to be** like lava to the undead. We'll be **safe** here."

"I'm just happy to see **some animals** for a change," Emerald said. **"Here, boy!"** She got off her horse and approached a small red animal. It almost looked like a wolf. As she drew closer, the creature **scampered off** into the ferns.

"I wonder if they can be **tamed?**" Ophelia asked.

Max and Lola were crouching before a wispy white flower. "Hey, is that **meadowsdown?**" Lola asked. "And **morningwhisker! Wow!** I'd say this forest is an alchemist's dream come true!"

Stump was like me: totally **speechless,** looking around in awe. **"D-d-dude."**

Elric smiled at him. "The first time I saw the silverwood, my face must have looked just like yours." He went back to his horse. **"All right,** everyone. **Glimfrost** lies on the other end of the valley. **Let's ride!"**

And we rode.

Glimfrost
Moon Elf Village

That's what greeted us.

Although it was **technically** a village, that word seemed inappropriate—if not **insulting.**

As the Aetherian Knights dismounted, the glow of their lanterns had nothing on the moonstone lights. Of course, their lanterns were not held to provide **illumination,** but to signal **respect,** a way to greet honored friends.

The greeting **was not returned.** . . .

The village was certainly **beautiful,** yes. Elegant, **breathtaking,** enchanting. **But it was also empty. Abandoned.** Not a moon elf in sight. The only sounds were **the echoes of our footsteps** on a type of stone I didn't recognize. The silence was **unsettling.**

"They must have left for **Nepheridyll,**" Elric said. "That's the largest **elven city,** to the west of here. Although I do not suspect anyone still remains, we must **make sure.**" He turned to us. "Would you care to **assist us** in the search?"

Eight villagers nodded in unison.

No. **Seven.** Lola was now studying a light blue flower, its petals embedded with **tiny metallic cubes.** I think it was some kind of ore flower. I've only heard of them. Ore flowers are the **subject of tales** told by old blacksmiths on warm summer nights, their eyes gleaming with not only the light of a nearby furnace **but with hope:** the hope to obtain some of **the legendary metals** such flowers are said to contain. That's all nonsense, though. The only metal **this** flower contained was **iron.**

Breeze's father seemed to be staring at me when he said, "**Remember what I told you.**"

"We'll stay close," Breeze said.

"And behave yourselves." Brio added. "We are guests—**not looters.** Otherwise . . ."

I finished his sentence for him. "You'll make sure the majority of our time training in the capital involves **mushroom stew.**"

He smirked. "Count on it."

Max was already wandering off, book and quill in hand. He seemed to be **taking notes,** jotting something down with every **unusual sight.**

"Figures," Cog muttered, and ran after him. "**Hey!** Egghead! **Wait up!**"

The rest of us trailed after them, looking in **wonder** at the bizarre village filled with **ghostly green light.**

Breeze was lagging behind. Before catching up to us, she turned back again, just for a second. She'd been looking at **one house in particular.**

We **ran up** every staircase, across every bridge, and through every house.

Most of the homes were **empty.** The elves had cleared out most of their item chests before leaving.

We stopped in front of an **armor shop,** the only store we'd seen so far. It had a simple design compared to the rest of the buildings. I guess whoever owned it wasn't an elf. A sign outside read:

The Unicorn
Tank in Style

Cog walked up to the door. "There's gotta be some stuff in here. No way the shopkeeper was able to **haul off everything,** eh?"

"Remember what her dad told us," Ophelia said. "We aren't here to **loot.**"

Emerald drew closer to her. "Pretty **honorable** there, Ophelia. Especially for someone who doesn't have **any** armor."

The **former waitress** glanced down at her outfit. She crossed her arms. "I will have **no part** in the **plundering** of an elven village."

"You sure?" Emerald drew closer still and all but whispered into her ear: "Bet you could find some **enchanted chain mail** in there. Nice stats. All **shiny. Full** durability."

Ophelia looked at her outfit once more. You could see the conflict in her eyes. The **internal struggle.** Which finally seemed to break as her shoulders sagged. "**Um** . . . I suppose we could see if there are a . . . few spare pieces we might . . . **borrow.** Yes. **Borrow.**" She raised her head. "Whatever we take, we will someday return. Is that **agreed?**"

Emerald nodded. And smiled. "**Yep.** Someday."

As one of the two **captains** present, I should have said something. But **honestly,** looking down at my own pitiful set of armor—armor all **rusted** and full of **negative enchantments** that would embarrass even a **noob**—I found it hard to say anything. In fact, I was the one to open the door. After all, the sign said "**tank in style.**" I like tanking in style. Who doesn't? Tanking hordes of zombies is **great and all,** but if you can't **look cool** while doing so, what's the point? I **did** have my reservations about the shop's name, though. **The Unicorn.** And once inside . . . my suspicions were confirmed and **my dreams absolutely crushed.**

Like Cog had guessed, it seemed like the shopkeeper had tried to take everything, but when that proved **impossible,** he'd left some stuff behind. **Scattered across the floor** were many different pieces of armor: tunics, boots, bracelets, bracers, helmets, and leggings, many of which were enchanted—with **good enchantments,** I might add. And this would have been **great news** for me, spectacular news, only . . . I'm **not a huge fan of** the color pink. Or violet. Or rainbows. Or pastel shades. Nor am I particularly fond of kittens, baby birds, bunnies, butterflies, unicorns, and seahorses . . .

I've said before that I'd be willing to wear **anything** so long as it had good stats. **I retract that statement now.** Truly, a line **does** exist, and that line was right in front of me. **No way was I going to cross it.**

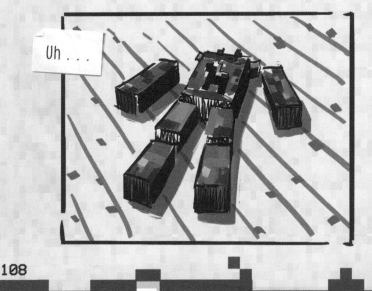

Uh . . .

Capes with hearts.
Kitten masks.
Unicorn mail.
What's not to like?

In what could be called **pure horror,** each boy present watched as the girls **tested out** different items, **whirling around** and asking **each other's opinions** on color scheme and so on. It was almost **enraging** that they seemed to prioritize each item's appearance over its stats. Didn't they know how to appreciate fine **enchantments?!** I've been hanging out with girls for a while now, and I **still** don't understand them! Breeze seemed to be the only one who had some appreciation for

the raw power that these outfits provided, and at least she picked one that didn't look like a costume from a children's play. The rest . . . **well,** to give you an idea, Emerald was wearing bracers that looked like **bunnies.** And a pair of fuzzy boots that **also** resembled bunnies. As for the other two, I . . . **no,** I can't go on. **Words escape me.**

"Well, maybe it's not a **total** loss," Max said. "Maybe we could **dye** some of that stuff."

"Dye or no dye, I'm not wearing something called **Mermaid Veil**," Stump said. "Or **Faerie Rainbow Cloak, Butterfly Bracelet** . . ."

"We could **rename** them," Cog said. "All we'd need is an anvil, and . . . **oh, what am I saying? It's hopeless.** Most of this stuff can't even be dyed anyway without a **super high** Crafting skill."

"Better luck next time, huh, guys?" Emerald said with a **wink.**

Stump let out a huge sigh. "Yeah, **yeah.** Enjoy your bunny slippers. The monsters will probably go for you first, since only a **noob** would wear something like that."

She walked up to him and **poked him** in the chest. "**Idiot!** They're enchanted with **Echo I!** Know what that does? It'll **slightly increase** the power of any songs I play!"

Stump raised his hands defensively. "Please don't hurt me with your magical songs boosted by magical bunny slippers! Songs you haven't even learned yet! **P-p-please! N-n-no!**"

She poked him again. "There's a song that can **heal,** remember? **You're** the one who wants to become some kind of **tank!** Think your health bar's gonna stay up all on its own? What if you run out of potions? Who's gonna be there to **heal you? Noob!** I was thinking about **you!"**

"Oh . . . well, I feel like a jerk now."

"Hurrmph!"

All right, so they weren't totally ignoring the enchantments. Maybe **I'm just bitter.** But it's fine. My time will come. Someday, we'll come across a **real** armor shop. A shop run by an **Underlord.** They're these guys that wear **black felsteel** plate and command the undead. I saw an entry on them in Max's *Encyclopedia of the Undead.* Actually, at this point, I'd settle for any set of armor that isn't sparkly or doesn't resemble **a rainbow fish.** Is that too much to ask?

A potion was lying on the counter, and Cog grabbed it, taking a sip. **"Not bad."** It was a flavored drink—**moonberry juice.** A white hat was also sitting on the counter, and he grabbed this item as well, throwing it on. "I'll go check on the knights." He headed for the door, turning back one last time and tipping **his new hat** as he did.

After we left the shop, it seemed my luck was only **growing worse:** Emerald found **a bow.** An **OP** one, too. It was just sitting in some random chest. Why couldn't it have been **a greatsword** or something? Upon opening that chest, her eyes **grew wide,** and she let out a small gasp. "**Wow! This is amaz**—**zzingly useless! Yep!** I'd better carry it, then! Wouldn't want **this** piece of junk **clogging up** anyone's inventory space!"

MOONHEART BOW

ENCHANTED

HASTE I: +10% ATTACK SPEED
WOUNDING XV: +150% CRITICAL DAMAGE
FROSTBOLT I: ON-HIT EFFECT, COLD-BASED,
5% CHANCE TO IMMOBILIZE TARGET FOR 2 SECONDS

Moonheart? I wouldn't have used it, anyway.

"That should go to **Breeze,**" Max said. He lowered his glasses and gave Emerald the **stern look** a teacher gives an **unruly student.** "It's only **logical.** She's the only one here who's **any good** with a bow."

"Yeah? Well how about **this** logic," Emerald said. "With this **OP bow,** I'll be just as good as her! Why put all of your eggs in **the same inventory?**"

"It's fine," Breeze called out. **She can keep it.**

She was nearby, in one of the many gazebo-like buildings that were scattered throughout the village, standing on a balcony that overlooked the silverwood.

I wanted to ask why she was being **so glum,** but the scene in front of her made me totally forget. The silverwood stretched far to the west—**unbelievably** far—and from up where we were, with an open view, the tops of the trees looked almost like the ocean. . . .

You could see the mountain range perfectly from here. **The Spines of Ao.** No map could have ever done justice to its size, nor could any view but this one.

Only then I did understand how truly **enormous** that range really is . . . and only then did I realize how **hard** it would be to climb any of those mountains. With vast sheer cliffs whole biomes in height, and windswept valleys packed deep with snow, reaching any of those peaks seemed **impossible.** Suddenly, I remembered **Pebble. . . .**

"That temple must be up there somewhere," I said, joining Breeze on the balcony. "Did he know how hard that climb was going to be? He must have known, right?"

Of course the others gathering around us didn't understand a thing. I'd already told them about **Urf** yesterday. How he'd attacked us. But they hadn't yet heard about **Pebble's quest** to trek to the top of one of these mountains. It was time to tell them.

"I always knew Pebble wasn't such a **bad guy,**" Emerald said. "**Stressed out?** Definitely. **Troubled?** Maybe. But a monster? **No way.**"

"I overheard the knights talking about those mountains," Max said. "According to them, the foothills are **crawling** with undead. The nastier types, too. **Ghouls. Wights.** Even one that can turn you into stone with **a single touch.**"

As if I didn't feel **bad enough.**

115

Our journey so far has been like **a birthday party** compared to what Pebble must be going through. At least he's with that **S** guy. Surely they wouldn't start climbing without being prepared, and I think I remember some people in **Owl's Reach** talking about a shop that had a sale on **Cold Protection** gear. Or am I just imagining things to make myself **feel better?**

"We could head there now," Stump said. "With us helping out, we could **light** that beacon and be back **in time for enderscones!**"

"I'd love to," I said, "but I doubt the knights would go for it. **Besides,** do you think we'd even be able to get there in time? Well, maybe with Swiftness potions . . ."

"There's no need to **worry about him,**" Max said. "Remember that look he always had during **our exercises** in school? **Such focus.** He's survived this far—I doubt he'll fail now."

Without looking back at us, Breeze nodded. "**I agree.** His main weakness used to be his confidence. It got in his way. **He was careless.** That's how I was able to **defeat him** in our duel way back. But when I saw him a few days ago, he no longer seemed like that. He was . . . less **reckless** than before."

So she noticed that too, I thought, but I said nothing.

Ophelia joined Breeze at the rail. "Just hope he comes back. Villagetown could use him."

"That's something I've been thinking about," I said. "Fifteen of us are going to the capital, right? What if there's another attack? We won't be there."

"I think it'll be fine," Max said. "Breeze's dad is staying, as is most of the Legion. And recently, there just haven't been as many attacks. The Eyeless One said he'd be back, but so far he hasn't."

"Yeah."

Still at the rail, I looked out at the mountains again. In one particular little spot—a shadowy cleft not too far below the tallest peak—I saw a flicker of golden light. Almost like that area had been illuminated, briefly, by more than a thousand torches. I strained to see another flash but saw nothing else, only shadow. . . .

Emerald joined us at the rail. "It is a lovely view," she said. "Look at that river. Hmm, no boats by the dock. I wonder if the elves sailed away?" She turned to the rest. "Anyone up for a swim? The knights won't care if we leave the village, right?"

Cog was returning as she said this. "Don't think they'll even notice. They're poring over **a journal** some moon elf left behind. Seems like they've **discovered something important.** They wouldn't tell me what it is, though."

"Then we're off!" Emerald said. When no one **followed** her, she turned back. "**What?** The river's just past the wall. **We'll be fine.**"

In this scene, I'm contemplating my future, Cog is staring at something far away, Ophelia is whispering something to a blushing Stump, Breeze is gazing at her reflection while touching an ear, and . . . Max and Lola are holding hands???

Okay, so we not only **looted** a bunch of stuff but also listened to Emerald and wandered off, **past the wall.**

We **were** in sight of the village, though, and there was nothing else out here besides **a few strange animals.** One was small and gray with

119

black rings around its eyes, and another was dark brown and larger than any cow, with some **fearsome-looking** horns. For a long time, we just sat on the dock, taking in the beautiful and otherworldly view while chatting. There was nothing else to do but wait. The knights were still reading **those scrolls,** and the horses had hardly recovered **half their endurance.**

"Y'know, guys, I think **I've figured it all out,**" Emerald said. "About our world, I mean. Okay, so the Terrarians are always arguing about whether or not our world is **actually real,** right? Well, Kolb said that, on **that game server of theirs,** you used to be able to ride a horse forever. I mean **forever.** Horses had no endurance to speak of. They just **couldn't get tired.** Then the server changed the rules. **An update,** I think it's called. Anyway, after this, the horses suddenly had endurance to make them **more real.**

"And that's not the only thing that suddenly changed in their game world. There were tons of **little modifications** here and there, right? Every month, or every couple of months, a new update **there,** new update **here,** and now **stormberries** exist, with tons of crafting recipes for them. . . ."

120

Stump seemed very lost. "Emerald? Please tell me you have a point."

"My point is this: Their game was constantly changing. One day, there was no endersteel armor. The next day, there was. But our world has never been like that. It's always been the same."

"That's an interesting observation," Max said. "Maybe you should become a philosopher."

"Whatever. It has to mean something."

"You can say our world isn't changing," Stump said, "but what about Villagetown? Bumbi tried making a house of cake! Cake, Emerald! Cake!"

Emerald sighed at him. "That's . . . not what I meant. I meant the laws, the rules, you know? Oh, forget it. . . ."

I was trying to understand what she was talking about, but after Stump mentioned Villagetown, I couldn't stop myself from asking what I'd missed back home. He replied so fast and with such excitement that I could tell that he'd been waiting for this moment. The words poured out like water from a broken dam. . . .

"First, Leaf discovered how to craft greatswords," he said, "and then Winter found an owl, then Drill found a secret underground chamber with an iron golem that was trying to **craft pizza** . . . or maybe Winter found the owl first. Oh, and the Legionnaires recruited a new member, **a girl named Rubinia**—she's kinda **weird.** Oh, oh, and the ice cream shop has a new flavor! **Powder keg,** it's called. It's really **delicious!** They called it powder keg because the flavors burst in your mouth! It's gray like a smoke cloud with bits of chocolate cake crumbs. Oh, we also **explored the Overworld** a little bit, and we slept in an underground house. We helped the Legionnaires make some **beacons.** They're like these towers that we can see from far away so we won't get lost. We also traded for some new weapons like **my war hammer** here and **my shield,** because I wanna be **a tank** like Emerald said, maybe a Knight, but maybe starting as a Warrior first, though." He paused only to **take a breath.** "Oh, and **an ocelot** showed up at our village! A **bluuuuuue** one!"

"Nice." Emerald rolled her eyes at him. "Way to **ruin the surprise, nooblet.**"

"Yes, we were hoping to surprise you," Breeze said. "Oh well. Guess I might as well tell you. We ran across him while scouting the Overworld. It sounds like he's **bound to the quest,** too."

122

I laughed. "What? You mean this ocelot can talk?"

"Yeah," Emerald said. "I know. Villagetown is apparently a hot spot for craziness."

"You know, I'm not even that shocked," I said. "I've already seen and heard so much these days. So there's a blue ocelot who can talk." I shrugged. "Why not? I've already seen a shape-shifting zombie-slash-ghost. Oh, and Kolb's a hero from a fairy tale. So why not this, too? And maybe Stump is secretly an enderman whose real name is Eggbert? Again: Why not?"

Everyone turned to Stump, who sputtered: "W-what are you talking about? What ghost?!"

I then told them about the thing that attacked us yesterday, and Breeze admitted she'd already been hunted before. After she and her father escaped, they had nowhere to go, because Shadowbrook was in ruins. So they wandered the Overworld aimlessly, traveling from inn to inn, village to village, at times sheltering in the wild. No matter where they went, though, someone (or something) was always on their tail. One time, it was a pigman in black robes; he had a dagger imbued with Wither XII. Another time, it was a shadowy form, like a ghost, that **slowly emerged** from a wall, reaching for Breeze while she was on her bed in her nightgown, writing in **her diary.** Not **at all** creepy. No wonder she's always so **withdrawn**—the poor girl must be **traumatized** after all the things she's been through. **I'm** gonna have nightmares just **hearing** about that.

Stump, on the other hand, was more interested in the dagger: **"Wither XII?!"**

Breeze shrugged. "That's what my father said. He studied that weapon for days. The poison was **so strong** that it had actually eaten away at the blade. It barely looked like the blade of a dagger. And the weapon itself had a **maximum** durability of one."

"So it'd break upon striking anything," Max said. "A kind of **one-use** item with a **serious punch.**" He had **the same look** as when he'd inspected the silverwood's exotic flowers. "Where is it **now?**"

"Think my father still has it," she said. Still sitting on the edge of the dock, she **stared down** into the water. "Anyway, we should assume that **the Eyeless One** has learned what we've learned. Since we're all **close,** it's possible that his servants will come for you, too—if only to **anger us,** to get to us. The capital is a **very large city.** It will be easy for someone to **blend in** there. For an **assassin.** Like my father's told me again and **again** . . . we'll never be **safe,** even at the foot of the king's throne."

They all fell **silent.**

It was **a lot to digest.**

Bound by blood. The **descendants** of heroes. What makes us **so special . . . ?**

Not only do we have to go through **rigorous** training and study up in **the Academy,** we also have to **watch out for . . .** whatever they are.

No one said a word for the longest time. Everyone was **thinking,** staring ahead, watching the clouds roll by or the waves on the river. There was **a slight wind.** Every time the leaves rustled overhead, **I looked up.**

Minutes later, the wind **really picked up,** and the branches above the dock were all but shaking. Just like me. I stared upward, expecting **the worst.** When the wind rushed through the forest again, the **weirdest** sound came from just down the river, almost like a bat or something, **except louder.**

Keee-uuu . . .

I literally **flew up** one block **while sitting down.** No idea how I managed that. I looked around, trying to see what made that noise, and I **jumped again** as that sound rang out once more.

Keee-uuuuuuuu . . .
Kee-kee-kee-kee-kee-kee-kee!

I shot to my feet, as did **everyone else** except Lola and Breeze.

Ophelia drew her sword, Emerald **took cover** behind Stump, Max **hid** behind Emerald, and Cog, holding onto his bottle of juice, **crouched** behind Max.

"What's that **sound?**" Lola asked, evidently **unafraid.**

"I think it's **a blockbird,**" Breeze said. She pointed at one of the **large violet bushes** not too far away.

Suddenly, **I saw it.** Just down the river, on top of that bush, sat a **reddish, cube-like form.** I ran. I ran with the speed of an enderman who'd just been invited to a pool party. I ran **so fast** that I stumbled into Cog, who cried out in that **screechy voice** of his: "**Runt! You little noob!**" I made him **spill** his moonberry juice. That's how **excited** I was at the thought of seeing a **blockbird.** I had only heard of them until today, and I had to see if they really were just **tiny feathered blocks with wings.** Nothing would have prevented me from reaching this goal. **NOTHIGN.** I know, I spelled "nothing" wrong there, but that was on purpose to try and capture **my excitement.**

A blockbird

There it was, **in its nest,** exactly like **I'd imagined.**

All of my friends were running up to me now, and soon they joined me in **staring at** this bizarre animal. Ever seen eight villagers standing on top of a bush? I'm not even **going to try** drawing it.

"It sounds **angry,**" Lola said, petting the bird's head.

Breeze knelt down. "That's because its nest is **almost broken.**"

"**Oh dear.**" For once, Lola **wasn't smiling.** "I suppose we should **craft a new one** then, shouldn't we?"

"And I suppose you know **the crafting recipe** for a **bird's nest,**" I said—having forgotten how **foolish** it is to doubt **the ever-so-talented** Lola Diamondcube.

Her smile **returned.**

Of course her smile returned.

"As a matter of fact," she said, "**I most certainly do.**"

RECIPE FOR BIRD'S NEST

You most certainly have to be kidding me.

In less than a minute, Lola crafted a **brand-new** nest with her own two hands and replaced the blockbird's old nest. Soon, the blockbird was no longer chirping in an **annoying** way, but **singing.** It went something like this:

Kee-kuu-kee-kuu-kuu-kee,
kee-kuu-kuu-kee-kuu . . .

Uh, I think that's pretty much **all of it.** If there was more, I forgot.
Only then did it **hit me.**

WHAT IF I TOLD YOU

LOLA DIDN'T USE
A CRAFTING TABLE

"Lola, um . . . **how did you craft that nest?**"

"Isn't it **neat?** It's my ability," she said. "**Artisan.** It lets me craft
any 3x3 item without using a crafting table. I thought it
might **come in handy** if we ever need to craft something **in the heat**
of battle. **Rubinia** taught me."

130

Of course.

While I was out in the Overworld doing my thing, my friends were **doing things too.** Including learning **new abilities.** Basic ones, like mine, but they're all still **requirements** for whatever type of **class** they've thought about becoming.

Stump

SHIELD BASH

THROWING UP A SHIELD AND SMASHING INTO BAD GUYS HAS NEVER BEEN MORE FUN!

Emerald

PILFER

LOOK! FREE ITEMS! A 100% DISCOUNT! SO LONG AS YOU DON'T GET CAUGHT.

Lola

ARTISAN

WHAT? DIDN'T YOU KNOW? CRAFTING TABLES ARE SO LAST YEAR.

Max

FAMILIAR

IT'S A PET! IT'S A MINION!
AND A MOST LOYAL ONE, TOO.
AT LEAST, UNTIL YOU
FORGET TO FEED IT.

Ophelia

PARRY

SHIELDS? PSH! WITHOUT
THE SOUND OF TWO BLADES
CLASHING, YOU CAN'T CALL
IT A BATTLE!

133

HIDE

EVER SEEN A THIEF WITHOUT THIS? IF YOU HAVE, YOU SAW A BAD ONE!

"Kolb told me that's what makes someone **elite** or not," Emerald said. "**Abilities,** being able to do **more** than just swing weapons and place blocks. After all, every monster out there has at least **one kind of trick.** It's almost **humiliating,** huh? All this time we've been without any **cool attacks!** In a way, that's like being **beneath a slime. . . .**"

She certainly had a point. **Without abilities,** a person is as simple as **Urg the Barbarian** who—in his words—can only "atak bad things" and "eet good things." That's all Urg does, **atak bad things** and **eet good things.** And truth be told, Urg's not even that great at *eeting* good things—or even *eeting* things at all, for that matter—as evidenced on **page thirty-three** of **volume VII** of his series:

134

"Oog! Me hungy!
But where green thing go?
Me want eet!
But where go???"

"Where go???"

"Hungy?" Hmm. I think that ties with "noobery" as my favorite new word!

At any rate, we need to be less like the **pigman** above and more like the monsters we face. Creepers are feared for their **ability to ruin** your house. Endermen for their **ability to teleport** into your bedroom any time they want. If we really are supposed to help save this world—or even protect our own village—we have to get on their level.

And lately, **we have been.**

Now, we're **duel wielding, sneaking** around and **stealing** stuff, and **crafting items** without the use of any crafting tables.

And that's just the start! So if any of Herobrine's minion-noobs just happen to be reading, be warned: Watch your back, nooblings, and be very, very afraid!

We are no longer peasants scared of simple wooden swords! We're on the path to nobility, to perfection that will make even the fancy lords jealous!

"I do say, noble sir, ye have bested me in this duel."

"Thy abilities are most exquisite."

WHAT IF I TOLD YOU

ABILITIES ARE REALLY COOL

"Watch this," Stump said.

Along with an **enchanted iron shield,** he was brandishing a **huge war hammer.** He charged at a spruce tree, his shield raised in front, and **slammed** into the trunk. This **special attack** was so **powerful** that the spruce tree actually shook. Such is the power of **Shield Bash.**

As for Max, he has **a pet bat** named **Chompy.** It's a **special** type of pet, controlled through his **Familiar** ability. It has a weak **bite attack** and can be sent flying ahead to **scout** dangerous locations. It can also

137

carry one item with its little clawed feet. The uses for this delivery bat are limited only by one's imagination, I suppose. . . . For example, it could carry **healing potions** to wounded allies. Anyway, know that calling a familiar is **the first step** for any aspiring **magician.**

Max raised his hand and sent **Chompy** fluttering into the sky. All it took was the flick of a wrist to change his pet's direction, and before long, the bat was **rolling** and **diving** . . . and nearly **clipping Emerald's hair.**

"Hurrmph! You know, I'm still looking for a good reason to try out this **new bow!**"

The bat, returning to Max's shoulder, **squeaked pitifully.**

Having put away his shield and hammer, Stump **rummaged** through his belt pouch. "**Huh.** Thought I still had one of those muffins."

Emerald hastily brushed off a few **sparkling crumbs** from her tunic.

That was about the time Breeze's father came for us. He didn't seem angry; he didn't even seem to **notice** the new outfits. He simply strode up to us with a **grim expression.** More grim than **usual,** at least.

"Come. **We must leave at once.**"

No one said much of anything as we **returned** to the horses. Not Elric, not the grumpy knight Zigurd. We just **saddled up** and **left.**

Obviously, they'd learned about **something bad.** I knew it was something to do with **why the elves left.** Maybe it was about **that keep. Stormgarden.** Maybe **an army** was gathering there. Breeze's dad told us it's in **the eastern wing** of Ravensong. We must have passed it this morning. But **we didn't encounter anything,** so I couldn't understand why everyone was **so worried.**

Stars started to appear across **the cold black sky.**

We rode **in silence,** stopping only to feed the horses the very last of the Swiftness potions. Then I saw something else I **couldn't understand.**

It was already morning again: Directly in front us, on the horizon, the sun was trying its best to shine through the heaviest bank of **fog.** That didn't make **any sense,** though, because we were riding **directly south.** Why was the sun rising **in the south** instead of **the east?** And why now? It had set only an hour ago.

But it wasn't the sun. . . . **I suppose I was in denial.**

My mind was **unwilling to accept the cold truth** in front of me.

After we passed that ridge . . .

I **vaguely** recall Emerald screaming, Ophelia shouting.

Everyone shouting.

It was **inconceivable**. **Villagetown**. Our village. **Burning**.

In places, the flames rose over **fifteen blocks**, stretching toward a sky **filled with ash** that was falling back down like **black snow**.

Every second was an hour as we galloped to **the wall**. I couldn't believe what I was seeing. As we reached the remains of **the north gate**, I spurred my horse inside.

Behind me, everyone was calling out, **telling me to come back**. I almost did. The flames were **sweeping through** the libraries, clouds of thick smoke formed **floating walls**, and the metallic sounds of battle came from **everywhere at once**. How cobblestone was **burning**, I didn't know. And I didn't know it was possible for **sand to smelt into glass** without the use of a furnace. It was **terrifying** to see even iron doors crumble under the **unnaturally red flames**. My horse started whinnying **furiously** and rearing up. I'd never before seen an animal **so terrified** by fire.

"Fine," I said, jumping off. "**Go**."

With a last whinny, the horse **immediately fled**.

"**Noobery . . .**" I drew **my blades**. "That's what I should have named you."

141

I was **running** now, sword in each hand, still unable to register the **destruction** around me. Everywhere I looked was a crumbling house. A burning wall. **A pile of debris.** A zombie to my left—I cut it down **without stopping,** just a little spin while running. A familiar hiss to my right, I dashed to the left. The monster exploded **without effect;** I was one block out of range.

As I **ran and ran,** the distant sounds of battle **never** ceased.

Sounds like it's coming from the square, I thought. *I want to help out, of course, but **my parents** . . . All right. First things first.*

I reached what was left of **Shadow Lane,** encountering **no one.** As I continued on my path, the flames were dancing left and right, and I couldn't see a thing beyond them. **A grayish red haze.** And the faint outlines of buildings wavering in the heat.

Which way? ***There,*** *I think.*

Although I couldn't see very well, that **didn't matter.** I knew these streets. **Instinct guided me home.**

They weren't here.

Jello was gone, too, so I figured they'd taken him and **evacuated** like everyone else.

But where? It was **impossible** to think—I was **just standing** in my burning house, mind **completely frozen.** I turned back to the front door to find there no longer was a front door, only flames.

As I rushed outside, **a zombie** emerged from the smoke to my left, and from the right came **a skeleton in full iron.** Without any effort or thought, I turned each into **piles of experience** that I didn't even bother to collect, leaving them to swirl behind with **the faint ring** of glass. . . .

More emerged from the clouds ahead, vague forms **with outstretched arms.** Whether they were zombies, husks, ghouls, or something worse, I **didn't notice** and **didn't care.** I didn't even look at them; I only saw them **falling** from the corner of my eye, like **puppets** with cut strings. It was as easy as harvesting seeds. But this changed as more emerged . . . **again and again.** Maybe they had been following me and were only now **catching up.** Or maybe they were drawn to the sound of **harvested experience,** which by this point was like continuously shattering glass.

Hopelessly **outnumbered,** my emotions took hold, and I flew into what I can only call **a noob rage**—swinging **wildly, recklessly,** and yeah, I know I'm being a little **melodramatic** right now. **I don't care.**

Dude, my village was under attack, and **my house** was on fire.

DIEEEEEEEEEEEE!

KILL ALL MONSTERS!
RRRRHHHHAAAAAA!

Then **something happened** that I still **can't explain.** The
diamond sword in my right hand **swung much harder** than it
should have. As though the weapon was **propelled by some external
force.** That's the only way I can describe it. At the same time, the blade
left behind **a violet trail.** The damage was **crazy. Twenty-five.**
Triple the average damage.

A husk's gray form crumpled like **a deflating balloon.**

I took in all of this within **a fraction of a second,** never ceasing to **swing** as the horde trudged **mercilessly** onward. Yet, I was losing ground. There were just **too many.** My back now pressed against a wall, I fought with everything I had . . . hoping the **mysterious** power would return.

Eventually, **it did.**

This time, there was **a sound like wool tearing** as the **obsidian blade** in my offhand swung with the weight of an anvil. Both a zombie and a ghoul fell to either side, like **practice dummies** to me.

As time went on, **these strikes** occurred **more frequently,** until at last I was **pushing them all back.** Whether from **confidence** or the same **mysterious force,** my movements became **faster,** more **graceful,** blades whirling before me. There were times when I delivered **two attacks** on either side **simultaneously.**

In this moment, **I was no longer a swordsman,** but the conductor of some **beautiful** song, controlling the battle's tempo with my swords instead of a baton. With each crescendo came an **arc of brilliant light** that scattered their front line, knocking them all away if not outright **destroying** them; with each **lull** came parries and sidesteps, stringing them all along, **drawing** them all in, and **lining** them all up for yet another **sweeping attack.**

Idiots.

That was too obvious.

Hmm . . . what are they doing over there?

At last, I found that I **no longer** had to drive them away. They began accomplishing this themselves. **They were retreating.**

At first, slight **backward movements** rippled through their ranks. Small waves of **doubt.** With each newly fallen, this turned into more of a blind panic, a . . . **stampede.** The word "**stampede**" almost seems like the wrong choice, because it brings to mind a herd of animals instead of hideous abominations. But that's what it looked like.

It was unbelievable, but **the horde** of scary undead beings **vanished** into the layers of drifting fog as quickly as it had arrived. The last to leave was **ghostlike.** This spectral entity looked like **tattered black wool,** and it lingered for a moment, **studying me**—its eyes like red coals in a pool of shadow—before **slithering off** through the air.

Just seeing that thing made me **shiver. An actual ghost.**
Somehow I could sense that it was **very old and powerful.** I
forgot about it when I looked down at **my blades.** Then I **burst
into laughter** and **jumped,** practically dancing with joy like a noob
probably does upon defeating **his first enderslime.**

What was that?!

What the Nether just happened?!

Whatever, I'll take it!

And when can I do it again?!

Oh, what am I doing wasting time like this?

I have to find Mom and Dad. . . .

A thundering of hooves drove me from my thoughts only
moments later. It was Sir Elric, followed by Breeze.

Breeze jumped from her horse and **stormed over** to me, looking
angrier than Emerald had been that time Stump ate a slice of her cake
project in Crafting I.

And she said the same thing Emerald had: "**What** were you
thinking?!"

"At least you didn't have to **save me,** right?"

"**Your parents are safe,**" Elric said. "Come. The square is on the brink of being **overrun.**" He glanced down at all of the **crude weapons** and other **random items** lying around. Stuff the undead had dropped. "Might I ask . . . what happened here?"

"**Um . . .**" I wanted to tell them, but how could I explain? "I guess they didn't like **the joke** I told them."

Elric raised an eyebrow. "As you say."

Breeze sighed at me. "**Where's your horse?**"

The enemy

Void fire, burning even the gravel

Legionnaires

When we arrived at **the square,** it looked like this.

On one side stood **a valiant line** of **noble heroes.** Knights. Legionnaires. Villagers.

On the other side stood **the enemy.** I couldn't make them out clearly in the fog, but they must have **outnumbered us** at least five to one.

The ones I'd fought were just **a small fraction** of what was found here.

The school was still standing, somehow. What **a miracle** that was, because everything else was . . . **gone.** That beautiful marble fountain?

Gone. The mushroom stand? **All gone.** *(Well that one actually didn't bother me too much.)* And the ice cream stand? Well, I couldn't see it from here as it was about **three hundred blocks to the west,** near the tree garden, but it was probably **gone too.** Oh, and my favorite food stand? The one I wrote about when I first introduced my school? The Lost Legion had turned that thing into **some kind of bunker.** There, people **were crafting** and, above all, brewing. At a time like this, **healing potions** were more **precious** than diamonds. You could trade a whole stack of endercarrots for one. Promise. If endercarrots actually existed, I mean. But **they don't.** Nope. Sorry to crush your dreams like that. And sorry, **this is a huge paragraph,** isn't it? What if I wrote **this whole diary** like this? **Just one big paragraph!** How far could you read without **going crazy,** or at least maybe getting angry? Like, dude, why hasn't Runt **ended the paragraph** yet? Will he? Will it **ever** end? Also why is Runt **the coolest** villager that ever existed? Okay, **I'll stop.** And now that you've read this far, you probably feel as angry as I felt when I realized that . . . **there would never** be any more ice cream ever again.

As I jumped off Breeze's horse, I quickly **wiped away a tear.** Which

only made things **worse,** because it reminded me of **ghast-tear swirl.** Oh,

the suffering these monsters have caused! **It's just too much . . . !**

·Runt!· Stump ran up to me. "Dude! I tried following you, but

my horse **panicked!"**

"You shouldn't have taken off like that!" Emerald said. "Do you have

any idea what kind of **crazy mobs** are out there right now?!"

I shrugged. "Are you guys not worried about your parents, or . . . ?"

"They're safe." That was Kolb, now approaching. "Well, as safe as

it gets, anyway, considering our current situation. Ophelia's friends took

everyone **down into the mine tunnels.** We have a new keep there."

Sure enough, besides Ophelia, no one from **Team All-Girls** was present.

I did spot most of **my former classmates,** though. Helmets

falling over their eyes, most in **mismatched armor** no doubt hastily

thrown on. Many of them **nodded** at me; half as many came up

and said something. I don't remember who said what. There were **too**

many voices and **questions** flying at me all at once. I **do,** however,

remember most of the things that were said. So keep in mind, each of

the following lines came from one of my former classmates:

"Runt?! Thank Entity **you're here!** Now something crazy is going to happen! **I just know it!**"

"Did you really find **an aeon forge?** Is it . . . going to **save us** . . . ?"

". . . Am I **safe** now?"

"**Dude**, Runt! The mayor was **nearly assassinated!** He's in the mines now, **with our parents.**"

"**Drill?** He's with **Kaeleb**, that **ocelot**, and a few others. They took off after some pigmen **in dark red robes.**"

"We managed to push them back. **For now.**"

". . . D-do you think we'll **m-make it?**"

"Runt, I don't really know what to say at a time like this, so I'll just say . . . **it's been real.**"

"**Nice sword**, Runt. Is that obsidian?"

"Runt! Is that **you?** What's up with that armor? It's all rusty. And that hat. Is that . . . **mold?!**"

"So how was **your quest,** anyway?!"

"Heard you ran into **Pebble.** How is he? Wish he was here. We could **really** use him."

154

"Stump said you saw **an elf.** Is it true? I hope to see one someday. I heard **moon elves** are found in silverwood biomes. And **dusk elves** are found along the coast."

"Hey man, you've missed some stuff around here. Someone's been planting a new type of tree in the tree garden. **Mossy oak.** I think those trees are normally found in rainforest biomes. I wonder who's been planting them?

"Hello, Runt. Question: Did you happen to encounter any **redstone steam golems** during your travels? I only ask because I heard they have those in **the capital.** Oh. You didn't go to the capital? **Sorry.** My mistake."

"Hey, Runt. Sorry to bother you again, but I just can't stop thinking about **that obsidian sword.** What kind of enchantments does that thing have? Can I see **the stats?**"

"**Runt!** It's been forever! So Stump said you found **a dungeon** that had more than one room? He was joking, right?"

"Um, why is everyone asking him so many questions right now? **I mean, hello?** We're facing imminent destruction, people! **Ready your shields!**"

That's about **all I can remember.**

If you feel **overwhelmed** by that wall of text, imagine how I felt.

(Oh, and that last line was Emerald. But you probably guessed that already.)

"Enough!" Kolb said. "Give him some space. He's been through a lot." He **rescued** me from the crowd and gave me a pat on the shoulder. **"Glad to see you,** kid. And hey, good work out there. Heard you managed to obtain **an aeon forge."** With a smile, he added, "Wish we could have met under different circumstances. We have so much to . . . **discuss."**

I glanced around, looking for Breeze. She was some ways away, speaking with **Elric** in private. Judging by their expressions, they were discussing **something serious.** No idea what.

I turned back to Kolb. "And what **is** the current situation?"

"Guess they realized it was **the perfect time** to attack, with so many of you gone. **The Nethermancers** burned away part of the wall with **their spells.** We took most of them out, though. Kaeleb **ambushed** several, chased after the rest who fled. Right now, there's **only one** left we really need to worry about. See that one over there? **That's the leader."**

Across the square, I saw **a figure** that stood several cubes taller than all the rest, encased in black plate adorned with **glowing red runes** and brandishing **a black sword** over two blocks in length. That armor was almost too much, though. Maybe too try-hard? Almost like he wanted the whole world to know that he's the **ultimate bad guy.** Actually, there's a villain in *Urg the Barbarian* who looks like him.

"He's an **Underlord?**" I asked.

"**He is.** Underneath all that plate is **an irontusk** highly trained in **the dark arts.** Most of the undead are **under his control.** He's our **main** target. Once he falls, this battle is **over.** But reaching him **will be difficult.** We'll have to clear a path through his minions. And no, **arrows are useless.**

157

His armor appears to be heavily enchanted against them—they just **bounce off.**"

"What's an **irontusk?**" Stump asked. "Are they like . . . pigmen?"

Zigurd **scowled.** "They're like pigmen, all right, only **twice as strong** and about a **hundred times harder to kill.** Hate those things."

"It seems we've really angered **the Eyeless One,**" Brio said. "As all of his previous attempts **failed,** he has employed some of **his most elite units** to ensure Villagetown's destruction."

Elric returned with Breeze at this point. The knight nodded. "Yet it is no great matter. This village is **still standing . . .** for we are still here." He turned to Kolb. "These are **truly dark times,** but know **the Knights of Aetheria** are honored to stand by your side. It could be said that we are in **great debt** to the Lost Legion. I do not know how many villages in the West were saved thanks to your order, but this number is most certainly great."

Kolb shook the knight's hand. "It is **our honor** as well." He turned to me. "**Hmm,** Runt. Those swords of yours are **almost broken.** You should repair up. There's **an anvil in the bunker.** And grab a few

H-llls while you're there. Don't forget milk, too. There's a shade in that army, high-level, spirit subtype. Those things can inflict a wide variety of nasty debuffs."

H-llls?

What's he—oh. Healing llls. Got it.

How'd he notice my swords are almost out of durability, anyway? He never misses anything. . . .

I tried by best to speak heroically like the knights around me: "It is my honor to assist in the coming battle." I bowed. "Sir."

It was one of those situations where you could either joke or cry, and I didn't want to be reminded of my favorite ice cream flavor anymore. Before I left to repair, I saw that Kolb wasn't wielding a broken sword. Across his back was a diamond greatsword—in perfect condition. Emerald claimed the other one is useless in its current state. He must have stashed it.

Upon seeing this place, I felt kind of sad. The food here used to be SO good.

I pounded away on an anvil in what used to be **a food stand.**

Both of my swords had almost **no durability** left. That's how much I'd fought earlier.

My head was a mess. It had all happened **so fast.** I focused on my items, trying to **take my mind off** everything.

Hmm. Definitely need to get stronger Unbreaking enchantments. Some better armor, too. Something that doesn't slow me down so much.

I'm really glad Breeze taught me Dual Wield. When facing swarms of low-level monsters, dual wielding is far better than using a shield: You need all the damage you can get.

*But what was that back there? **The light?** The extra damage? It was almost as if I'd used **some kind of ability.** But the only abilities I have are **Dual Wield** and **Analyze Monster**, right? So how was that possible? It doesn't really matter, I guess. The real question now is . . . how are we going to **pull through?***

I glanced at the other people inside the bunker. Two villagers and three Legionnaires stood on the other side, preparing potions or equipment. They were talking about the first battle. The one I'd heard, earlier. It had been **pretty intense,** according to them. **Many wounded.** They couldn't brew enough potions.

*Wish I'd been there for that. But I had to try finding Mom and Dad. **I hope they're okay.*** I kept hammering on my swords. *They must be scared, down in the mines. They'll be fine, though. **Ophelia's team** is protecting them. . . .*

As **the sparks jumped up** with each blow, Breeze stepped in.

Behind her was **the red-robed wizard girl, Rubinia,** who was, according to Stump, **an Enchanter.** Or is it **Enchantress?**

The Enchantress opened a nearby **item chest,** retrieved an unusual-looking sword, and handed it to Breeze. "I managed to place **every enchantment** you asked for."

SAPPHIRE KATANA

ENCHANTED

UNDERTOW

ATTACK SPEED 1.35

AVERAGE DAMAGE 11

THIS ITEM CONTAINS THE FOLLOWING ENCHANTMENTS:

HASTE II - WOUNDING II - UNBREAKING III

"It took me **forever** to get the **stats** right," Rubinia said. "I hope you like it. Oh, and here's **a new scabbard,** too."

"Thank you . . . **Rubinia.**" Tears almost welling in her eyes, Breeze fastened the scabbard to her belt and sheathed **her new sword.** She drew it again with **impressive** speed. The blade **sang** as she performed a basic thrust then **parried** an imaginary attack. "**Perfect.**" Upon sheathing this weapon once more, she **gave Rubinia a hug.** "You be careful out there, **okay?**"

Rubinia nodded. "I'm the one who should be saying that. **Take care,** Breeze."

After the Enchantress left, Breeze gave me a worried look. "How are you feeling?"

"Bad, of course. But we should have expected this, right? With us gone, it was the perfect time to attack."

"It was, but we'll be okay. I know we will. All we have to do is fight, as we've always fought." She drew her new blade. "Rubinia found it in the ruins of Shadowbrook. We became friends when she arrived, and she ended up giving this to me. One of the many things you missed while you were away. All of my armor is from Shadowbrook, too." She meant the stuff she grabbed from that shop earlier, which she was now wearing. "I wasn't going to take anything," she said, "but when I saw all this stuff from my village, I felt I had to."

I inspected her outfit. It had an almost somber appearance, but it reminded me of the ocean. Her gloves, boots, and long tunic were crafted of dyed shadowmoss that had been woven and enchanted, pretty much like wool. The rest—bracers, armlets, tiara, belt—were of many different materials. Coral. Seashell. Seastone. Various types of opals. Prismarine. Dark prismarine.

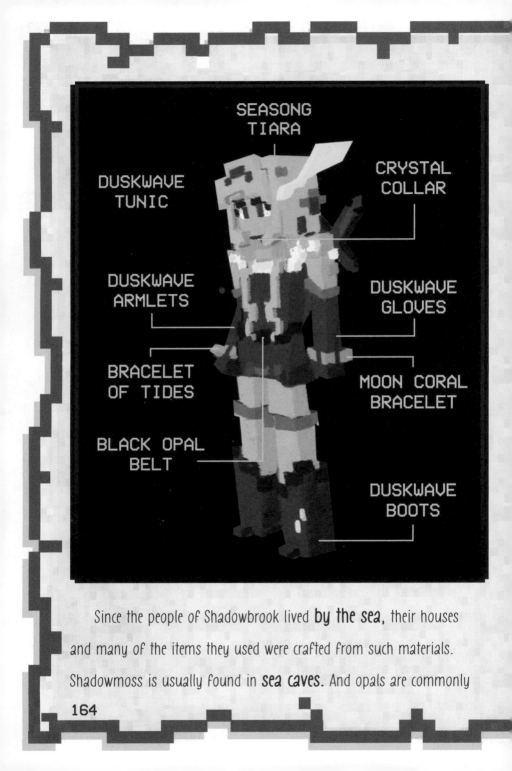

SEASONG
TIARA

DUSKWAVE
TUNIC

CRYSTAL
COLLAR

DUSKWAVE
ARMLETS

DUSKWAVE
GLOVES

BRACELET
OF TIDES

MOON CORAL
BRACELET

BLACK OPAL
BELT

DUSKWAVE
BOOTS

Since the people of Shadowbrook lived **by the sea,** their houses

and many of the items they used were crafted from such materials.

Shadowmoss is usually found in **sea caves.** And opals are commonly found by mining near the coasts. There are **seven different** types of opal, some more common than others. They're like diamonds or emeralds, pretty much, and they're used in a lot of **advanced crafting** recipes. Not like I knew all of that, though. Breeze told me.

She offered **her new sword** to me. "You want it? I almost feel **guilty** with all this new gear. Emerald **also** gave me **her new bow.**"

"No, it totally suits you," I said. "**And . . .**" I recalled how my swords had functioned earlier. Even though they weren't anything **special,** they were clearly working. I shook my head. "**Keep it.** I'll be fine with these." I glanced at the item chest. "Let's get some **supplies,** huh?"

I searched through the item chest, which was stocked with **Healing III potions** and **bottled milk.** That's normal milk, contained in a bottle instead of a bucket. It's said that most cows descended from a line of **enchanted cows** that once lived ages ago. Even today's cows have milk capable of **purging our system** of most minor magical effects, good or bad. I didn't have any milk on me, but even if I did, I would've taken some milk bottles anyway. Think about it. I'm supposedly **the descendant** of a villager hero who lived long ago, right? Well, what kind of **hero** drinks from **a bucket?!**

After we stashed several bottles each, **Brio** stepped in. "**Where'd you find that?**" he asked, meaning her armor.

"Some shop."

"I did say **no looting.** But never mind. I'm glad you did." He stepped closer. "**It looks good on you.** It's been so long since I've seen . . ." For the first time ever, he looked **despondent.** He couldn't speak. The armor she wore, of a type commonly seen on **Shadowbrook's female scouts,** was clearly bringing back a lot of **memories.** But her father soon regained his composure—**even smirked.** "Of course, I don't suppose you're going to let your . . . **friend** head off to battle without **something to match.**"

"What do you mean?" she asked.

"Runt has obtained **an aeon forge,** has he not? So let us forge. I still have Shadowbrook's old recipes on hand."

Brio held up **a massive tome.** It was larger than any book I'd ever seen in my life. He set it down on a nearby crafting table, and standing on either side of him, we watched him flip through **countless pages.** Each page contained **an advanced crafting recipe,** and roughly half of the recipes contained ingredients I'd never seen before—some I'd never even **heard** of. It reminded me of the times the Legionnaires talked about how many recipes there are. Over **ten thousand,** according to some.

"What would be **best** for him," Brio asked, "given the ingredients at hand?"

She thought for a moment. "**Hmm.** What about **redsteel?**"

"We don't have much time. It would take **hours** to smelt enough."

"**Oreweave?** No, we need raw ore for that. . . ." Breeze kept thinking. "Wait. How about **gemwrought mail?**"

"Not a bad idea," Brio said. "We certainly have enough opals." He turned to me. "We took **many different types** with us. Yet we haven't been able to use them until now. Every recipe that requires them is of an **advanced** pattern." He held out his hand. "**Forge,** please."

I retrieved the aeon forge from my inventory and handed it to him. I had no idea what gemwrought mail was, but it **sounded cool** and involved an advanced crafting table. I was **totally** on board. He placed the forge on the ground, next to the standard crafting table.

Then he retrieved a set of leather armor from that chest nearby. "What color would you prefer?" he asked.

My time had indeed come: "**Black.**"

He smiled. "Shadowbrook's **main color.** There's a reason why both **my daughter and myself** wear black. You would have fit right in."

He grabbed some black ink from the chest, threw each piece of leather onto the standard crafting table, and dyed the entire set black. He then meticulously placed the tunic on the forge, in the central square, before laying out **several different varieties of opal** in every square surrounding the tunic, all at different—yet specific—angles.

There was a **brilliant green flash,** just like when Max had tried crafting that staff back in the inn. And as before, columns of **pale blue light** sprang forth from each item. This time, however, there was an **iridescent** glow, and the gemstones suddenly **merged** into the armor. What remained **took my breath away.** It looked like a black leather tunic, all right—only, it was **embedded** with diamond-like shards. A suit of diamond or emerald plate is way too flashy for my tastes, but **this . . .**

Breeze's father picked the tunic up carefully, inspecting the result. "Not **my best** work," he said, "but far better than what you're currently wearing. Although it offers a level of protection somewhere between leather and diamond, it is **superior** to diamond overall. **Some abilities**

can only be performed in lighter armors such as this, and furthermore,
your **mobility** won't be affected, nor will stealth. It's also quite
receptive to enchantments."

He then crafted the remaining pieces. I **threw everything on,**
leaving my old armor in that chest. And for a moment there, clad in
a suit of armor that the people of Shadowbrook had proudly wore, I
almost felt like **a member of that village.**

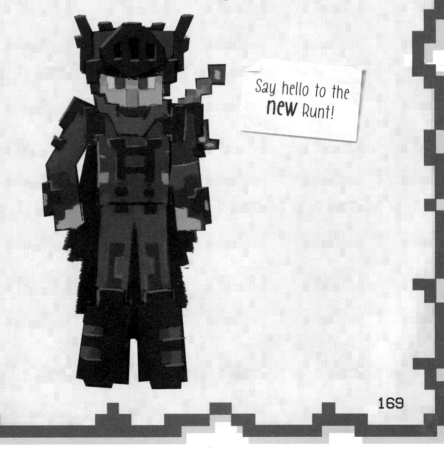

Say hello to the **new** Runt!

Brio smiled again. "Now you look like **the hero** you're **destined** to become." His smile faded. "My daughter . . . told me about **the undead** earlier." He stepped closer. "What happened, **exactly?**"

"Don't know," I said with a shrug. "I just . . . **fought way** better **than normal.**"

Breeze stepped closer, too. "Almost like you were using **abilities,** right? The same thing happened to me. Remember **the move** I used to **finish Urf?** Well, when we were **defending** Shadowbrook, I **accidentally** used that for the first time. It just kind of . . . **happened.**"

"Although our libraries indeed had **several tomes** capable of **transferring abilities** to the reader," Brio said, "she'd never read any of them. It seems she was **born with several abilities,** and I suspect the same can be said for you."

"**Huh.** I suppose there's no way I can easily find out what I have?"

"There isn't," Brio said. "Not until you **unlock** your **visual enchantment.** It took Breeze weeks to really understand what abilities she possessed. I—"

The door nearly **flew off its hinges** as Stump barged in, followed by Max and Cog. All of them were carrying **bundles** of crafting ingredients the Legionnaires had given them. Most of this stuff I didn't recognize.

Stump was all **puppy dog eyes.** "Kolb said you might **loan us the forge.** Just for a bit."

Brio **seemed amused.** "Did he now?"

"**He did.** He said the battle's **at a standstill,** and he said it might **make sense** for us to use this time **productively** by crafting some armor. He also said **you would be willing to help us.** Sir."

"It seems like he said **a lot** of things."

Before long, Breeze's father was once more over the forge, crafting away like some **legendary smith:** pounding **endersteel,** sawing aetherwood, shearing moonsilk. He could craft an item with **incredible speed.** He worked each object with such familiarity, without hesitation— as though he'd been crafting for **thousands of years.** When he struck a bar of endersteel with the forge's diamond hammer, the sparks that flew **shimmered** with ghostly hues, as if the sparks themselves were enchanted . . . and I imagined **Entity** must have looked like that, eons ago, when he began crafting **weapons of indescribable power. . . .**

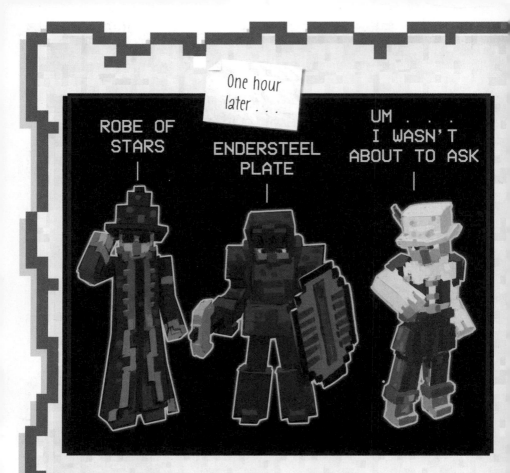

Well actually, it was more like ten minutes. I was just SO captivated watching him use that forge. I kept thinking about all the weapons I'd seen in that book of his.

"I c-can't **believe** I'm actually wearing **endersteel**," Stump said.

Cog looked at everyone's **rather somber** attire. "Shadowbrook must have been pretty **depressing** if everyone was rolling around in gear like this!"

Brio gave him **an icy look.** "Our village wore black as a way to show our **mourning.** We have battled against **the Eyeless One** for hundreds of years. **Destruction** and **sorrow** were all we knew."

"Didn't know he'd been around for **that long,**" I said.

"He hasn't. **His servants,** however, have. And they are the ones we have faced **through the generations.**" He paused. "**Oh,** I have something else for you. **One more remnant** of our past."

BATWING CLOAK
ACCESSORY—CAPE
ENCHANTED

THIS ITEM CONTAINS THE
FOLLOWING ENCHANTMENTS:

SWIFTNESS I

PROTECTION I

STEALTH I

REGENERATION II

FIRE PROTECTION V

"It's not the most **flattering** thing out there," he said, "but the stats are **much better** than the one you have on. You'll need some **fire resistance** for this battle."

"Some **seriously** depressing people," Cog muttered.

The cloak, designed to look like **a large gray bat wing,** did seem rather **gloomy** when paired with my armor, but I wasn't about to complain. **Those stats!**

Brio then held up **a dark red scarf.** "I almost forgot. **Kolb** wanted me to give you this."

Since I was being **showered** in items, my friends started getting **jealous** and began **pestering** Brio.

". . . G-got **any more** of those cloaks?!"

"**Yeah!** Where's ours?! **Hurrrg!** So unfair!"

"**Hmmmm.** I sure could use a **better** cloak myself."

"If you're going to craft anything, I'd like to assist."

I'll leave **you** to decide who said what. **A little game.** You should be able to tell **based on voice.**

Stump **whirled** around. "**Dude!** I feel like **a Knight of Aetheria!**"

"Thanks for the forge," Cog said to me. "Here, **buddy.** Have some

mushrooms." He stepped **super close** and handed me all sorts of

strange-looking mushrooms. Some were black with glowing purple

spots. Others were white with light red spots, bright orange with black spots, light gray with no spots, or light blue with rainbow spots. Then he handed me some . . . **plants?** They had blue stalks with transparent white bulbs on the end. "Found them in **Glimfrost,**" he whispered, **warily glancing** over his shoulder at Brio.

"And just what am I **supposed to do** with all this stuff?" I whispered back.

"No idea. But I need to free up some inventory space to stash my old armor."

·Hurgg.·

I put away the mushrooms and plants, and I picked up **the aeon forge.** "Hey, I—"

The door creaked open. **Always!** Every time it's the doors creaking or swinging open, cutting someone off! One of the younger knights, **Drest,** hurriedly stepped in and **bumped into** Breeze. "Oh, I'm sorry, Lady . . . **Breeze,** is it?" There was something **odd** about how he addressed her as **Lady** and **paused** before saying her name. He continued: "The enemy is displaying **unusual movement.** Sir Elric believes they will **soon** attack once more. He wants us to prepare for **the final wave.** And remember, **their leader** must be taken down at all costs."

I could already hear Kolb shouting from somewhere outside, delivering **a speech** to his **clan:**

"**Brothers and sisters,** although we've succumbed to infighting in the past, today we must put our beliefs aside. Today, I ask you to forget who you were and embrace **who you have become.** Regardless of what you believe, you are here, in a reality that cannot be fathomed, whose existence **must be faced.** Isn't that what you **secretly wished for?** There's no doubt in my mind that each of you here has **dreamed of this** in your past life. I know I did. Every time I logged in, I imagined what it would be like to live in **a world of fantasy.** To experience **real** adventure, where every action has meaning and **importance,** where others are truly counting on you. A world that truly does **need to be saved.** And now, that world lies before you. **Darkness** has spread across the land. Countless villages have fallen. The East **lies in ruins** and the West is soon to follow. From what we know, at least fifteen other clans have already **abandoned the idea** of defending this continent. Will you follow them, sailing north as they have? **Or will you follow me today, to victory?**"

At once, every member of his clan drew together and **shouted in**
unison:

"We are the Lost Legion!
We will **never** retreat!!!"

LOST LEGION
BATTLE SUITS

RUBY
EDGE

LEGION
BLADE

(BLACK, WHITE, AND RED
ARE THE CLAN'S COLORS)

RUBY
DAGGER

Let 'Em Know
Ballad of Villagetown

Written by Emerald

181

The war is right here
Like this endless eventide
Barely held them back
Desperately we vied

Don't let them win
Don't bend the knee

Be the heroes
straight out of prophecy

All the things that
used to own us

Can't scratch our
health at all

It's time for us to
test our skills

And reach the
record for most kills

Let 'em know
Let 'em know

We are known to
Make creepers cry

KITTEN MASK

EXCALIBUR BLADE

LEGENDARY GREATSWORD
(NON-UNIQUE)

AVERAGE DAMAGE 25

STORM V
(15% CHANCE OF EXTRA LIGHTNING DAMAGE)

STONE II
(2% CHANCE OF TURNING TARGET INTO STONE)

EMPOWER III
(BOOSTS ALL MELEE ABILITIES BY 30%)

SUNDER VII
(IGNORES 70% OF TARGET'S ARMOR)

WOUNDING X
(INCREASES CRITICAL STRIKE DAMAGE BY 100%)

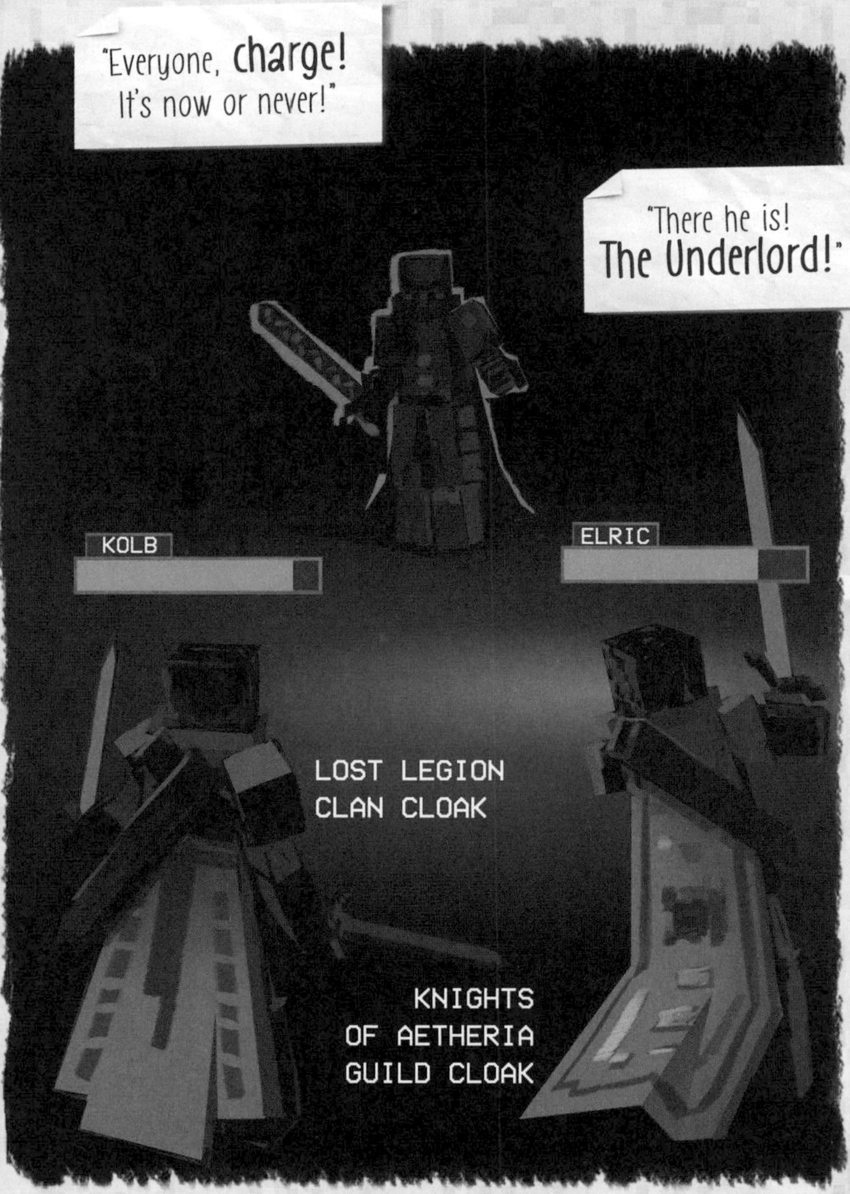

"Everyone, **charge!** It's now or never!"

"There he is! **The Underlord!**"

KOLB

ELRIC

LOST LEGION CLAN CLOAK

KNIGHTS OF AETHERIA GUILD CLOAK

Our weapons sunder
Through the boss
With a huge sound

UNDERLORD

Runt's swords are leaving
Little cube-like wisp
Trails all around

He one-shots what appears to be some kind of ghast

HAUNT

DEEP, HEROIC VOICE
He looks so good in black!
That gear must be
His laaaaaaaast!!!

Let 'em know
Let 'em know
That we fought
till the
Brink of dawn
DEFLECT
FLAME BLAST
Let 'em know
Let 'em know
The simple noobs
are gone . . .

Poof!
"Huh? Where'd he go?"

As we closed in to **finish off their leader,** he dashed for cover behind his minions and then **ran away.**

Breeze drew **her bow** and chased after him. Elric grabbed her by the elbow, telling her it was **too dangerous,** but she broke free.

"**Go**," Kolb said to me. After dispatching some more undead, he tossed a **Swiftness III** potion at me. "We'll hold the line."

I ran while chugging and caught up to her by the time **the speed boost** started to fade.

In the light of early morning, we chased **the Underlord** all the way to one of Villagetown's vast meadows, near the tree garden where Breeze and I **first met.**

There wasn't much smoke here, only gray walls far away, like **impending storm clouds.** Across the meadow—at least one hundred blocks away—the Underlord had almost reached the trees.

As Breeze pulled back **an arrow,** I told myself it was **pointless.** The Underlord's armor made him all but immune to arrows. But the arrow she pulled back was **obsidian,** likely picked up from the battlefield earlier. There had been **lots** of skeletal archers lurking out there, their arrows **enchanted with various debuffs.** And this arrow contained **Wither II** along with **Catscratch V.**

Catscratch is nasty. With a successful **critical hit,** it increases the effect of any debuffs the target has—by one point per power level. The Underlord's armor only protected against **physical damage,** not against any debuffs an arrow might bring. It **didn't matter** if that arrow only did one point. As long as she landed a critical hit, the payload would strike—**Wither II** would become **Wither VII.**

Still, it looked like an **impossible** shot. I could barely see him now, just a black speck growing smaller every second.

Breeze took **a deep breath.** Time seemed to freeze completely as I watched her aim. And as it froze, I noted **the scent** of fresh air, the grass sparkling with cubelets of dew, the mud puddles on the surfaces of dirt blocks, shining from last night's rain . . . all of this was at odds with **the devastation** beyond.

"You've got this," I said.

She shrugged. "Maybe."

Just kidding. She didn't shrug, and neither of us said anything.

What kind of **noobs** do you take us for? That would have **thrown off** her aim.

Ziff!

The arrow sped through the sky, **arcing gracefully.** The most beautiful shot I'd ever seen. It vanished into **the shadows of the grove** where the Underlord had just fled.

We ran to the trees, through the flowers and tall grass. The garden had changed since I'd last seen it. Someone really had planted **mossy oak trees.** In places, you couldn't see any bark, only moss.

In the grass, illuminated by rays of sunlight, was **the Underlord's sword,** armor, and an **enormous** pile of experience. As we approached, the armor and sword crumbled into black dust with **a hiss. The crystal orbs** slid across the grass, toward **their rightful owner.** I wondered just **how much experience** she'd gained.

"I guess you **got him,**" I said. "**Nice work.**"

"Yeah. **It was a . . .**" She **shivered.** "Good shot, **huh?** Mostly **luck,** though."

"**Hey? What's wrong?**"

She'd **shivered** like that before. That's when I understood, and time suddenly stopped again. I realized **where she'd found** the arrow. She **hadn't** picked it up off the ground earlier.

She'd pulled it
from her own shoulder.

Breeze was affected by **Wither II.**

That shouldn't have been **a problem.** We both had a way **to remove this debuff.**

We'd taken a **few bottles of milk** from that chest. All she had to do was chug, and all status effects **would disappear.** But the bottle she now held did not contain milk. She popped the cork on an **H-III** instead. Her health bar **jumped up.**

I didn't understand.

Although the healing potion countered **the damage dealt** by Wither, it didn't **remove the effect** itself. Why didn't she just drink some **milk?**

She **shivered** again.

My thoughts **swirled around** as she drank another. An **H‑II,** this time.

"Breeze, **um . . .** maybe it would be best if you tried one of those . . . **other** potions. You know, **the white ones.**"

"**No.** Listen, I've never told you this before, but I . . . um . . . I get **really** sick when I drink milk."

". . . Never heard of **something like that.**" I glanced at her health bar. "**How sick,** exactly?"

". . ."

No reply.

I watched her drink potions of **Healing I, II, and III** for the longest time.

Then she **ran out.** The Wither still remained, endlessly grinding away at her **life force.**

"It has **an extended duration,**" she said. "It has to wear off, though. Another minute at **most . . .**"

With a **sigh,** I handed her **my own healing potions,** which she drank one after another. This, of course, only delayed **the inevitable.**

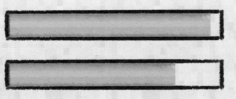

What is this **nonsense?**

"Can you just **drink some milk?"**

"I'll be fine," she said. "It'll **wear off.** I'm sure of it."

Finally, every last bit of food we had went toward keeping her health up. **Stormberry rolls. Enderscones.** Then we were down to the basics: bread and a single potato. Actually, I'm not sure how that got into my inventory.

"No muffins?" she asked.

"We're out. **Of everything."** I paused. **"Hey.** Are you telling me a bottle of milk will make you **more sick** than consuming **all that?"**

". . ."

I held up a milk bottle. "Drink."

"I can't."

"Breeze. Seriously. What are you doing?"

She turned away. "Runt? Can you do me a favor?"

"What?"

"I need you to go."

"W-what are you talking about?!"

"Can you just give me some time alone?"

Time alone? What in the Overworld? She has maybe a minute before . . . !

"Breeze, this is insane! What are you doing?!" I shoved the milk bottle in her direction. "Just drink, already! Drink!"

"Listen to me. I just . . . need to be alone. I'll be okay."

". . ."

"I'll force you to drink if I have to."

She whirled around, anger flashing across her face. "You're really stubborn, you know that?!"

215

"When it concerns **the health of my friends,** yes, I am rather stubborn."

Crossing her arms, she turned around again. **"Hmmph!"**

"Well?"

"Can you just go?"

"And leave you here **by yourself** with almost no health. What if something shows up?"

"Fine."

She raised **a gloved hand.**

Suddenly, she was surrounded by **a cloud of smoke.**

I didn't bother waiting for it **to fade.** I knew she'd activated **that ability** of hers and was **running off.** So I ran through the cloud, further into the garden.

Unfortunately, I had no way of knowing which direction she'd gone. That ability turned her **invisible** for a short period of time. **Five seconds,** I think she said. And she barely made **any noise,** even while running. There were three paths through the trees, so I picked one **at random,** depending on **blind luck** to guide me. Maybe I'd be able to spot her once her invisibility wore off.

My mind churned **even faster** than my legs.

*Why did she react **so strangely**? Why didn't she want to remove her status effects? She must be **hiding** something.* **But what?**

As I sprinted through a section of tall grass, I—

"Oof . . !!"
"Gahhh . . . !!"

—ran **straight into her.**

Both of us went flying in opposite directions and landed on our backs.

A potion was on the ground in front of me, glass sparkling in the sunlight. She'd been holding that. I'd **knocked it out of her hands.** I didn't pay much attention to it, though—I was focused on **her health bar** and felt so relieved when I saw she was no longer affected by Wither. She must have **downed some milk** after she took off. She was still extremely injured, **though. . . .**

She shot up from the ground immediately and **darted** into the shadow of a tree, where she remained.

"**Breeze?** Um, **are you okay?**"

"I'm fine. **Obviously.** Can you go? **Please . . ."**

I stood up and stepped forward. "**Seriously.** What's going **on** with you? Why are you acting **so weird?!"**

"I need to be alone."

"Yeah, **okay.** Well, we need to get you healed first."

I remembered the potion she'd dropped, turned around, and **reached for it.** As I did, I recalled her stating she didn't have any more healing potions. And truly, **the potion** at my feet wasn't capable of healing **anything.** I picked it up.

Disguise II . . . ?!

. . . ?!

. . . ?!?!

(?!?!?!?!)

I'd only read about **this effect.** We were going to try making some **Disguise I** potions in class, but that was **scrapped.** Someone had taken all of **the required ingredients** from the school's supply chests. . . .

I **tried to remember** what little I knew.

At first power level, it could make you **appear** as a different person, though a person of the same race. At second power level, you could appear as **almost anyone**—from a dwarf to a mushroom man. That depended on the potion's variant, which was set, through use of **extra ingredients,** just before brewing.

And this potion was of *the villager variant.* . . .

What the **Nether . . . ?!**

What's she doing with this . . . ?!

I whirled around. She was still there, in the shadows.

"You weren't supposed to **find out,**" she said. "Not until later." **She sighed.** "My father's going to be **furious. . . ."**

Peering into the gloom where she was **hidden,** I began to sense there was something **different** about her. Although I couldn't quite tell what. Her hair color was the same, the eyes, the armor . . .

She stepped **into the light.**

Even then, I didn't **notice immediately.**

But once I did . . .

In this instant, so many things **made sense.** Why she **never fit in,** why it had been so hard for her to **make new friends** at school. Why she knew **so much history.** How she recognized the sound of a **blockbird.** And suddenly, I knew who'd been planting **all the saplings.** Enveloped in sunlight, surrounded by **moss-covered trees** only found along the coast, **she looked completely** at home.

I couldn't **move.** I couldn't **speak.** I couldn't do anything but **stare.**

It's not like she **turned into a monster.** It was the **smallest** of changes, really. **Long ears.** A face that was **marginally more slender.** A slightly different **skin tone.**

That was it.
But it meant so much.

As I **gaped** in total shock, a part of me **feared** that things would never be the same. Another part felt **betrayed.** It's funny how even **the slightest difference** can mean **everything. . . .**

Since **Disguise** was **an illusion,** there had never been an icon to indicate the effect. All illusions are like this. The **zombie-ghost** didn't have an icon either. It'd be **too easy** to see through illusions, otherwise. An ability so basic as **Analyze Monster** would render them **useless.**

"**No more secrets,**" I finally said. "No more games, no more lies. **What are you?**"

221

She lowered her head. "Our **true name,** in the Sylvan language, is **Iaoao E'aeai.** It translates to **children of the cove.** You'd know of us as **dusk elves.** That's what we call ourselves, now."

"**Dusk elves . . .** I thought **Shadowbrook** was a village?"

"**It was.** But as you've seen, **not every** village is inhabited by those like you."

"Why **hide** from us?"

"We didn't want to **endanger** Villagetown. **Alyss** was my name. **My old name.** I changed it thanks to **an enchanted name tag.**"

". . ."

". . ."

". . ."

I'd **suspected** something all along. **Not this,** but something. After all, I'd **never** heard of a villager who didn't know how to joke around. And I've never known one to be so **skilled** in **shooting bows** and **riding horses.**

"**I'll tell you everything,**" she said. "After the battle's **over.**"

I was struggling not to **lose it.** "You're going to return to battle with **health like that?**"

"Um . . . no. I guess not."

Looking through my inventory, I retrieved all that stuff Cog gave me. **What about these?** Can we make stew or something with them?"

"Hmm . . . I'm not sure. Let me check. I have **my grandma's craftbook.**"

She held up an **ancient-looking** red book. *Grandma Eo's Craftbook.* It had various crafting recipes for food items, most using a **5x5 pattern.** There was only one recipe that used the ingredients on hand. **"Morel Medley."** Ghost morels—the black mushrooms—were the **main ingredient.** A souped-up version of mushroom stew. **Great.** I gave away all my food earlier, and now I was **starving.**

RECIPE FOR
Morel Medley
FROM THE KITCHEN OF
Grandma Eo

| 8x ghost morel |
| 4x fire fungus |
| 4x rainbow cap |
| 4x astral toadstool |
| 4x umber stalk |
| 1x bowl (acacia for better flavor) |

Arrange all ingredients so that they're facing north, and in the center of each square.

PROVIDES

AND THE FOLLOWING BUFFS:

After I **placed the forge,** Breeze began crafting away, though **more slowly** than her father. And . . . I'm ashamed to admit this, but . . . **a wonderful aroma** filled the air.

She held up a bowl filled with **something that resembled stew.** "Wanna try?"

"**Uhhhhh . . .**"

It's mushroom stew, I thought. ***Don't let** the aroma deceive you!*

She took **a sip.** "It's good. **Really.**"

Don't do it. Just don't. But my food bar was about to begin **dancing.** As hard as it is to believe, I took a sip. And it really **was amazing.**

One bowl restores your food bar **completely** and heals **five hearts.** It also provides the **Omnessence** buff, increasing experience gain, along with a buff called **Bounty of the Forest,** which increases strength by one, and finally a third buff, **Savory Hearth,** which makes one immune to the Chill effect. Oh, and all of this lasts for **three hours.**

"**Advanced crafting,** where have you been all my life?!" I said.

After giving me **another sip,** Breeze offered a third, but I declined. "**Your health** still has a ways to go."

"It's fine. We have enough for **one more.**" She smiled. "It's good, **right?** My grandma used to make this when I was little."

"**To be honest,** that stew's **so delicious** that even if I were **completely full,** I'd run laps around the tree garden just to reduce my food bar and eat **some more.**"

She made another, for me this time. And I **almost finished it.** But there was a **slight wind,** and **the shadows** behind her started moving, **changing.** Within them were **two glowing red eyes.**

It was **the shadowy being** from earlier. **Black claws** raked her shoulder, removing **a small fraction of her health.** Then she **fell** to one knee and remained like that, as if pulled to the ground **by intense gravity.** She was affected by **Stun.** With her **out of the fight,** the ghostly apparition turned **to me.**

You know
what <u>happened next.</u>

They say a picture
is worth a thousand
words. . . .

Somehow, as I fought this thing, I wasn't stunned. Instead, I was affected by **Slowness II, Weakness, Nausea V, Blindness, Mining Fatigue, Silence, Bad Luck VIII,** and something called **Curse of Icehollow.** Each time the shadowy being struck me, the damage wasn't **all that high,** but it inflicted **one of these status effects.** Seemingly at random.

I don't know **how** I brought that thing down. **A miracle.** In the end, I was affected by nearly **every negative status effect known to villager . . .** and **then** some. I can't even begin to describe how bad I felt, affected by all of this stuff—it took **three bottles of milk** to remove everything. That **Curse of Icehollow** was the last to go.

Breeze was fine. Her **Stun** wore off by the time I reached her. Trying to ignore **those ridiculous ears,** I pulled her to her feet.

"**How'd** you break free?" she asked.

"What?"

"While you were fighting, **you were stunned as well.**"

"Um . . ."

"I saw **the icon.** Although briefly. It vanished in **a fraction** of a second."

"I don't remember."

"And **your slowness** wore off at the same time. I've heard of an ability that can **clear any immobilizing effects.** You must have used that."

"We really need to get to **the capital.**"

"**Definitely.** It's . . . tiring, not knowing anything about ourselves."

I turned to the edge of the garden. The faint **sounds of battle** were still audible. "C'mon. Let's help them **clean up.**"

"Hey! **Wait up!**" As we left, she drank one of those Disguise potions. There was **a puff** of deep red smoke.

**When it cleared,
she was back to <u>her normal</u>
villager self.**

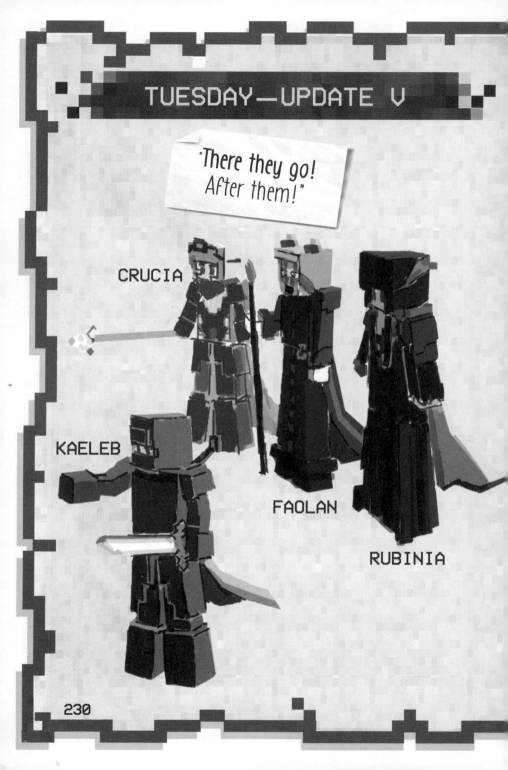

"The southwest quarter is clear. The remaining undead have been destroyed."

The undead fell **easily** without their master. **The Underlord** had several different aura abilities that **empowered** his minions. **Without him,** they collapsed like **sugarcane.**

According to Sir Elric, that specific Underlord was **sixth in command.** Just five steps below **good ole No Pupils himself.** One of his **dark apprentices.** So today could be called **a major victory. . . .**

As we cleared the last, it started **raining** again. It was enough to put the last of the fires out. With **our village secured,** I ran to the mines. Everyone was there. **Safe and sound.** Including **my parents.** They said a bunch of things I don't want to write in here. You know, the kind of things parents **typically** say to a son who just helped defend their home village from an attack. Oh, all right—I mean stuff like:

"Oh, look at **our little swordsman**—he's leveling up so fast!"

"Actually, I don't think I **have** leveled up," I told them. "We need to learn how to do that in—**oh, whatever.**" I gave them **a hug.**

The mayor **isn't doing so well,** though. He took an arrow coated in **Poison V** and **Frostwisp Venom.** Milk has had no effect on the latter. **The good news** is at least the venom isn't damaging him, but it's put him into a kind of **magical slumber.** Breeze's father claims there's a potion called **Cleansing** that can remove almost any status effect. He just needs **the ingredients.**

Oh, by the way, **Jello** is okay! My parents brought him along to the mine. He's eaten nothing but bread-based food items since I left, so when he saw me, he started jumping around **like a redstone spring toy.** Not that I've ever seen one of those things myself, but Max said he knows how to craft them.

We spent the rest of the day **rebuilding.** The wall, mostly. I was placed on **a different building team** than all of my friends, so I haven't had the chance to ask Breeze any more about . . . **that.** As I threw down block after block of cobblestone, **I couldn't stop thinking about it:** The image of Breeze standing in the tree garden kept **resurfacing.** Now that I know **what she really is,** maybe she'll finally start telling me more about herself. I'm sure the dusk elves have a very interesting story to tell.

Oh.

I finally saw the . . . **blue thing.**

" . . . "

"Hi."

He was just returning from a **"hunt."** He looks like **an ocelot,** kind of. A **monstrous** one. And his name is **Eeebs.** Yes, **he can talk.** Talking animals just . . . **weird me out.** I've been **avoiding** him ever since he first spoke to me. I'm sure I'll **warm up** to him. Just give me time. So many things have happened lately. I just wanted to come back home and **relax** for a bit, you know? **Oh, Runt!** You're the descendant of some **ancient villager hero!** You're going to be **hunted** by extremely creepy undead things that give you **every debuff** in existence! One of your best friends **is actually an elf!** Oh, and your bedroom?! **Totally blown up!**

Seriously, just leave me alone already . . . !

Finally, I ran into **Faolan,** the **wolf guy** I met in that dungeon. He was there in the battle against the Underlord, using his magic to **freeze the zombie minions** into ice cubes.

He smiled. "**We meet again.**"

I peered at him **suspiciously.** "How'd you get here so fast?!"

"A wise magician never reveals **his greatest tricks.**" He bowed. "Although I wish to speak further, **your leader is ill.** To cure his affliction, the necessary ingredients must be gathered. I wish you **good fortune,** my friend."

He left without waiting for a response. "**Um . . . see ya.**"

Late this afternoon, Drill asked me to **help Brio** rebuild part of **the village hall.** Since it's a huge building and was mostly undamaged, it's where everyone will be **sleeping** tonight. Rebuilding the outer wall was our top priority. We'll work on the houses tomorrow.

I couldn't help but wonder what he really looked like under that disguise. . . .

APPELLATE
GOWN

Brio slammed down **a block of quartz.** "Hot today," he said, wiping his brow. "By the way . . . **good work** out there."

"**Thanks.** You too." I threw down a block myself. "So the mayor . . . he'll recover?"

"**He'll be fine.** To brew **Cleansing potions,** we only need aetherspring. It's a **rare flower.** Typically found in **swamp** biomes.

Faolan and the Legionnaire **Kaeleb** have already set out in search of some." He placed another block. "So . . . my daughter told me **you defeated a shade.**"

"It **followed us.** I think it watched us throughout the battle, lingering, waiting for the perfect time to **strike.**"

"**Indeed.** Shades are **highly** intelligent, a powerful form of undead. Even I wouldn't have an easy time with one. That you defeated one by yourself, well . . . **that's quite a feat.**"

"What does that mean?"

"I suppose it means **the Prophecy** is true after all." He paused. "I also heard that you've . . . **learned of us.**"

"I won't tell anyone."

"It doesn't matter. I'll be revealing **the truth** at tonight's meeting. **No more hiding.** It's time **everyone** knew."

"Sir . . ." *(I wasn't mocking him. I was really trying to show respect.)* "When I fought **that shade,** I was hit with a status effect called **Curse of Icehollow.** The venom affecting the mayor is also related to the cold. Is there **a connection?**"

"There is. **A frostwisp** is . . . like a floating jellyfish.

238

Extremely dangerous, as all beings native to Icehollow. Icehollow is the common name for Icerahn, the fourteenth realm."

"Realm?"

"Dimension." He sat down on one of the blocks that served as a crenellation. That's a fancy word for one of the castle-like things on the edge of the roof. You know what I mean.

I sat down on one next to him, and he continued:

"After he fell during the final battle, the Unseeing Wizard was not completely destroyed. He had a protective enchantment in place that transferred his spirit to a phylactery, otherwise called a soulcrystal. The location of this crystal was soon discovered after the war ended, in Icehollow. The Knights of Aetheria launched an expedition to this realm and ultimately found what appeared to be a violet gemstone five blocks in height, which was surrounded by his minions in the process of performing a ritual that, once completed, would revive their master fully. . . . The knights defeated these servants. Yet the crystal could not be moved or destroyed by any known means. So they encased it within layers of bedrock and built a fortress around it, a remote outpost they continually manned. This was to prevent any of his servants from attempting to **revive him** again. For thousands of years, it worked. Alas, his servants, once **scattered** to the four corners of the Overworld, **regrouped.** They slowly grew in strength and number, and they returned to Icehollow, where they launched an attack upon the outpost. Many knights fell that day. . . . In fact, their order was **nearly dissolved.** Today, the Knights of Aetheria are just a shadow of their former selves. They are **strong,** even now, but they were **so much stronger** then. . . ."

". . ."

And **today** I learned where Breeze gets **her passion** for history. I can see why, too. It **was** a really interesting story.

"At any rate, you can associate the word **'Icehollow'** with the Eyeless One himself, since that is **his home world.** The wisest among my kind was convinced he'd built **a new castle** there, shortly after his revival."

"So we'll have to **go there.**"

"**Someday.** And that is why, when I began to realize that **the Prophecy is indeed true,** I felt only sorrow for **my daughter. And for you.**" For the second time in recent memory, he **looked quite**

240

sad. "You must understand that what you've faced so far is just the beginning. No matter where you go, they will always be hunting you."

Down below, where the mayor once gave his speeches, people were already gathering.

"If I may borrow the forge again," Brio said. "Village tradition calls for cake during any meeting, and today I will craft cake the likes of which these people have never seen."

STORMBERRY

FIREBERRY

MOONBERRY

As the sun fell, Brio, acting as **substitute mayor,** talked about **our victory.** How well everyone did. How the monsters won't **dare** return after the lesson we gave them. How the mayor will **get better** soon. And how fifteen of Villagetown's **finest young cadets** will be heading to **the capital.** A ceremony in our honor will take place in a few days, the night before we leave. As he spoke, **I ate cake** like everyone else, but **not just any** cake. What Brio made earlier **surpassed** even my newfound love for mushroom stew.

The temporary mayor continued:

". . . And I would like to thank **the Legionnaires.** The school caught on fire at one point, but they had the presence of mind to use **Waterburst arrows** to put the fires out." Those are arrows that create **a spring of water** upon contact, like dumping out a bucket. At this news, there was a round of **applause.** "Finally, there's one more thing I'd like to discuss," Brio added. "It will **shock you. I apologize** in advance."

"We never meant to **deceive you,**" Breeze said. "Only **protect you.**"

Together they took out **bottles of milk** and drank them before the crowd.

Before **a stupefied audience,** Brio shared the story of **the dusk elves,** their history, who they were, why they wore black, and where they **really** came from. . . .

"Although we once lived in **Shadowbrook,** that village was not our true home. We originally came from **an island far to the northeast. The Isle of Ioae.** Upon its shores, sheltered within **a vast cove,** was our city of the same name. Alas, our kind was all but **eradicated.** We have always been viewed as **a threat,** and that has never changed. Even now, **the Unseeing Wizard** searches for us. For we carry **relics** and knowledge passed down through the ages, both of which can help **defeat him.**" He paused. "Long ago, I was known as **Ezael Stormblood,** high retainer of **the noble Nightcrest family.**" He gestured to Breeze. "And she . . . was once known as **Lady Alyss Nightcrest. Countess of loae.**"

Silence.

*So that's why Elric is *so polite* to her,* I thought.

I **staggered** up to Breeze like a heavily damaged iron golem.

"You're . . . **some kind of princess?**"

She shook her head. "In our society, **a countess** wasn't very significant. And it doesn't matter, anymore. There's nothing left of **loae.** The entire island is **in ruins,** and . . ."

"Although she was once considered **minor nobility,**" Brio said, "I believe she is currently the highest-ranking noble among our kind **still alive** today. Most of us **perished** during the destruction of loae, including every last member of **the royal family** and every major house. . . ."

"And that is why she has **supporters** in the West," Elric said. "And why I have been assigned to **personally escort** her to the capital."

"So **you knew**," I said.

"Yes. Just as I knew she was keeping **her identity secret** for a reason. I had no right to reveal it." He smiled. "Although many in the West do not believe in **the Prophecy,** there are a few who feel she can **rally** the remaining **dusk elves** to our side." His smile faded. He stepped toward her. "Do you think this is **possible?**"

Breeze glanced down, **bit** her lip. "I don't think so."

"It is **unlikely,**" Brio said, "They chose to **abandon** our old ways. They blamed **the royal family** for Ioae's destruction. It was our king who asked many of us to learn of **ancient knowledge,** which ultimately drew the wrath of **the Eyeless One.** I don't believe they want anything to do with **the war.**"

Elric nodded. "Perhaps you are right. But I feel we should **at least** try. If she is willing, of course."

"**Wait,**" Stump said. "So Brio . . . **isn't** . . . your father?"

"Not my real father," Breeze said, "but I've always **thought of him** that way. My real father **fell** in a duel with an **Underlord** shortly after I was born."

Now I understand why she was *so insistent* on chasing after that Underlord. . . .

"I swore to **her mother** that I would protect her," Brio said. "And I have. As **Ioae** fell into the sea, I escaped with her in my arms, and we **sailed away,** as others did. . . ."

". . ."

". . ."

So Breeze is **not only an elf,** she's **a noble member of some fallen elf kingdom?** Among the last of a race that has—in Brio's words—only known **destruction** and **sorrow?** Okay, despite everything I learned lately, that was a lot to **take in.** I **actually** leaned against Stump. **My faithful friend** was just as shocked as I was.

"We need **ice cream,**" he said.

I nodded. "We do."

Kolb gripped Brio's shoulder. He talked a bit differently, like the knights. He was totally playing the part: "**A tragic story.** I am sorry for everything that has happened. And I swear on **my sword** that we will put an end to **the Eyeless One.** But regardless of how much you've lost, know that you have **family** here, and not only among the Lost Legion. These villagers are **counting on you.** I'm sure they won't mind following you while the mayor recovers. You've helped so much."

Emerald stepped in between the two of them. "Although I've **never** seen elves before, Brio has never let us down. He was hard on us in school, sure, but he's seen firsthand what **No Eyes** is capable of. He knew what was necessary for **our own survival.** We wouldn't have made it through today without him, **I'm sure of it.**" She flashed a **brilliant smile.** "Besides, he's the person behind **those wonderful cakes!** Eat a slice and tell me he's not every bit a villager as us!"

The villagers needed no real **convincing;** he was already like a second mayor at this point. Within moments, almost all of them were rushing up to him and Breeze to ask **all kinds of questions.** A few were even trying to **touch their ears.**

Puddles emerged from the crowd of villagers, **beaming** at Lola and Ophelia with outstretched arms. "Ready to work on your **gowns?!** Tomorrow night, we're having **another dance** in light of our victory! Think of it as **a final farewell** before all of you . . ." He wiped away a tear. "During your stay in **Aetheria City,** you'll need to dress properly . . . the gowns you'll be wearing are the latest fashion there."

He **smiled again.** "Sir Elric himself will be **advising** me on how to craft them!"

"I will also be showing you **a few traditional dances** of the West," Elric said. "You will need to learn them, if you wish to **fit in.**"

Breeze was suddenly whisked away.

When **the elf** returned *(man, it feels weird referring to her as that),* she looked completely **out of this world.**

"I still can't believe you're **an elf,**" Emerald said. "I mean, I knew you were **different,** but not **this** different. Hey, um . . . are **your ears,** like . . . **normal** ears?"

"If this is what people in the capital dress like, I already feel like Urg the Barbarian."

"Elf countess?" Cog muttered. "Pah! What next? Really? What?!" He bit into an enchanted stormberry muffin. "Amazing," he said to Stump. "Who cares about elves when stuff like this exists?! Can't believe that recipe of yours really worked! Hurrr! That silly forge is more useful than I thought it'd be!"

Stump held up a book. His mom's craftbook. "Wanna go craft some more?"

"You bet!"

"I'll be joining you guys," Max said. The twinkle in his eyes made me wonder if he was going to have another go at crafting a prismarine staff.

They didn't even ask
if I wanted to go.
Since I had the forge,
they literally just hauled me away.

Drill woke me up this morning. He was standing over my bed, **shouting** about how I'd be **working** with Emerald today. We had to run around the village all day, making sure everyone was building **properly** and helping out **where necessary.** Still in my pajamas—in fact, **still lying down** in bed—I gave him **a salute:**

"Sir! **Yes, sir!**"

I ate a quick breakfast, met up with Emerald, and we ran. As we did, I had this **weird** feeling that we were being followed . . . and yet **I didn't notice anyone. . . .**

"Noobery!
I'm a Knight of Aetheria, not some
builder! No, I don't want help! Wait.
Got any stormberry rolls?"

"Told you I saw a
zombie rabbit! **Now pay up!**
One thousand emeralds! We made a
bet, remember? Hey! **Get back here!!!**"

"Wanna hold him?
Runt? Hello? Hey!
Where are you going?!"

"Yes, this is an obsidian farm. No, I don't need any help. **It's dangerous work.** Go bug Emerald. **Oh!** Hey, Emerald."

So our village has survived **yet another attack.** Things started **calming down** by evening, with most of the **important** structures rebuilt. Just after sunset, I went to the observation tower with Breeze. We were **silent** at first, watching **the stars.** I was still having a hard time accepting **who she was.**

"The **Disguise** effect didn't change your hair color? Blue kind of **stands out,** you know."

"I already changed my hair," she said. "**Before.** It wasn't always blue. It was originally . . . **forget it. That was the old me.**"

"How'd you manage to change **your hair?**"

"There's a way to **permanently** alter your appearance," she said. "If you noticed, Sir Elric doesn't have the **typical** eyebrows of a male villager. Things like eyebrows, hair style, and hair color are **easy** to change. We couldn't alter our ears, though. You need so many **rare ingredients** for that. And we were **on the run.** So we decided to use potions. **A quick fix.**"

"Oh. Well, even if you didn't change that much, I don't think I'll **ever** get used to seeing you like that." I sighed. "Okay, what's the deal with the relics and **knowledge** your father mentioned?"

"He has **a keystone.** You need one to be able to travel to **the eighth realm** and those above it. And you've seen **that book of his.** It has every **advanced crafting recipe** and almost every **legendary one.**"

"**Legendary?** As in, more **advanced** than **advanced?**"

"**Yes.** And as for me, I **inherited** several items. You could call them **family heirlooms.**" She reached into her belt pouch, retrieving **a sword** from the **extradimensional space.** As one might expect, the blade was **black**—or very dark gray—and quite **long,** slightly **curved.** The hilt was made of **bone,** though darker than any type I'd ever seen. I could tell this weapon was **very old,** that it had passed through many hands until ending up in hers.

She handed the sword to me.

"It's a **legendary-tier weapon,**" she said. "One of two." She pulled **another sword** from her belt pouch. It was **similar** to the one I held, except with a hilt made of **grayish crystal.** "Although they're not among the **twelve weapons** Entity crafted, they're still **powerful.**

Or at least they were. They're missing **their gemstones.** Without them, they can't be **correctly** enchanted. I've never wielded either blade. My father said they should be **kept hidden** at all times. To be seen with such a weapon . . . would draw **far too much attention.**"

MORNINGTIDE
GREATEDGE
MATERIAL: BEDROCK, LUNAR CRYSTAL
ATTACK SPEED: 2.5
AVERAGE DAMAGE: 15
DURABILITY: 172 / 7,810
WATER AFFINITY
NEGATE I
[NEGATE CAN TEMPORARILY PREVENT AN OPPOSING
WEAPON'S ENCHANTMENTS FROM FUNCTIONING.]

EVENTIDE
GREATEDGE

MATERIAL: BEDROCK, DRAGONBONE
ATTACK SPEED: 2.5
AVERAGE DAMAGE: 15
DURABILITY: 255 / 7,810
SHADOW AFFINITY
LIFESTEAL I
[LIFESTEAL DRAINS A SMALL AMOUNT OF HEALTH WITH EACH STRIKE, WHICH HEALS THE WIELDER.]

"Their durability's **really low**," I said. "Have you ever tried **repairing** them?"

"You mean on **an anvil?** No. **A legendary weapon** can't be repaired that way. Only **re-crafted** on a forge. And we never had access to one. **Lately,** I mean. There were several in **Ioae,** but they were lost."

"Well, we have one **now.** Although . . . to re-craft, I guess we'd need the **proper materials.**"

"**I have everything.** Both blades are made of **bedrock.** The hilt of yours is **dragonbone.** Mine, **lunar crystal.**"

"**Uhh** . . . The way you said '**yours**' almost made it sound like . . . you're **giving this to me.**"

"**I am.**"

"And here I thought today couldn't get **any weirder.** Wait . . . where did you get **bedrock?** And **dragonbone?** And what's **lunar crystal?** Doesn't lunar mean **moon?** And dude . . . how can bedrock even be **mined?!**"

"We were **once** capable of many things."

"**Clearly.**"

"**Well?** Should we try **re-crafting** them? It should be pretty straightforward. From what I've read, we only have to place each blade on the forge, **overlay the materials,** and . . . I think **that's it.**"

I set down the sword she gave me, grabbed the forge, and placed it on the floor of the sky tower. "Let's **craft.** Err, **re-craft.**"

With a flash of **blue-green** light, both bedrock and dragonbone **merged** with the sword. The weapon now had **full** durability. **Five times that of diamond.** It was slightly smaller than the standard greatsword, and despite the blade being made of bedrock and over one block long, it was **lighter** than I expected.

She **drew closer** and pointed at **the edge** of my blade. "See how the cube pieces are just a bit **smaller** than a normal item? All **legendary weapons** are like that—they're made of slightly **more cubes.** This provides greater **strength** and **flexibility.** From what little I know about them, they were made during the **Second Great War** by our greatest smith, **Oaeo.**"

"**Oaeo?** What's up with all the **strange names?**"

"Dusk elves from my grandmother's time and before had **Sylvan names,** and Sylvan only uses **vowels.** Anyway, Oaeo became inspired to craft these weapons, like a kind of **madness,** and locked himself up in his tower for weeks to **craft obsessively,** barely sleeping, eating, or drinking. These weapons were **his ultimate expression.** He chose to craft each blade out of bedrock because weapons back then, especially ones made for use in the war, had to be strong enough to withstand **intense punishment.** Monsters were **much** stronger then, and the force that comes with powerful abilities can **destroy** ordinary weapons with ease. . . ."

I raised a hand **defensively.** "Please, no more! I'm **excited enough** as it is. I'm about ready to **charge** outside the village in search of a spider just so I can **try this thing out!**"

We worked on **her sword** next. When she placed the lunar crystals onto the forge, I wanted to ask her again **where she got them.** I **didn't,** though. When someone gives you **an ancestral sword** belonging to dusk elf **nobility**—the "ultimate expression" of some legendary smith—you **don't** ask questions.

"It might be best to keep them **hidden** while we're in the capital," she said. "But we can work on them in **our spare time. A side** project. Without the proper gemstones, they won't be able to hold more than one **low-level** enchantment. We'll have to **trade** for new ones."

"What gemstones?"

"Frost opal. Void tesseract. Both aether and ethereal topaz. Fire lattice."

"You lost me at **'void tesseract.'**"

"They're all **extremely rare.** It will take a bit of searching, but maybe we can find some in the capital. It should have more than a few shops that **specialize in gems.**"

"Yeah . . ." I stared down at **my new sword,** then threw it in its scabbard and slung it across my back. "And hey . . . **thanks.** I almost don't want to **accept** this, but . . . I know you'd insist."

"We'll need all the help we can get."

"Suppose we will. I—"

A door didn't interrupt me this time. If one had, I would have **destroyed** it. There are no doors in the observation tower though, only a **tall ladder** going fifty blocks down, and right now came the *clunks* of someone **climbing up.**

Two people, actually. **Kolb and Emerald.**

"Guess we're still going to the capital," Emerald said **glumly.** "I thought maybe we'd get a pass on account of our village being blown up, but **nope.** We'll be staying here for a few days to help rebuild, but then **we're off.** Classes start soon, after all. And get this: Elric says we'll be wearing **uniforms** at the Academy." She **exhaled,** blowing her bangs upward. "**So lame.**"

"I'll be heading there myself," Kolb said. "But I'll be staying behind a bit longer to help out with the **full** rebuild. That'll take weeks." He approached, noting **the new weapons** slung across our backs. "**Interesting** blades. I know dusk elf craftsmanship when I see it. Nothing else **radiates** such sheer gloom." He grinned. "You two have been **holding out** on me, eh?"

"You're one to talk!" I said. "They told me about what **you've** been hiding."

"Ah. **Sorry,** Runt. I've been meaning to **tell you.**" He pulled a **sword** from the extradimensional space of his belt pouch. Only **half of its blade** remained, ending in a jagged, diagonal fracture. **Just like the legend said.** Light gray in color, the blade shimmered with a soft, almost **rainbow-like** shine: the **legendary metal** known as **adamant.**

"So that's **Critbringer?**" I asked.

CRITBRINGER
GREATSWORD

MATERIAL: ADAMANT
ATTACK SPEED: 3.5
AVERAGE DAMAGE: 4.5
DURABILITY: 3550 / 128,000
DULLNESS II
SLOWNESS II
UNBLOCKING III
"A BLADE THAT HAS FALLEN FAR,
VERY FAR, FROM ITS FORMER GLORY."

"Originally named **Aeon**," the Legionnaire said, "and renamed by **its former owner**, a Knight of Aetheria. In its current state, its damage is **pathetic**. One of the blade's **fragments** was in **a dungeon** not far from here. Only recently did we obtain it. Maybe I could **borrow** the forge when you're done with it?"

"**Here**," I said while handing it to him. "**I'm done**. And you can keep it. I won't need it. They say **every crafting room** in the Academy has one."

He nodded. "Once I'm finished, I'll hand it over to **your father**, Breeze. He's already started **an obsidian farm**. Soon, NPCs are going to be walking around **in obsidian plate**." He laughed. "Never thought I'd see the day!"

"**Aetherians**," Emerald whispered, elbowing him.

"Sorry. I keep forgetting. **Aetherian,** Terrarian. Aetherian, Ter—"

Clunk, clunk, clunk! Stump climbed up **the ladder.** It's no longer the doors creaking open; now it's the ladders clunking. Next time I pick a spot to **relax,** there won't be any doors or ladders or anything else that makes **a ton of noise.** On the plus side, my friend was looking pretty **dapper** in an exquisite red-and-gold suit. **What a sophisticated young lad!**

"They wanted us to come get you," he said.

Ophelia followed him up, looking **absolutely amazing** in a gown **comparable** to the one Breeze tried on yesterday, only sleeveless and with long white gloves. When she took his arm, **he blushed so hard** his face almost looked like a block of redstone: **"Th-the dance will begin** in . . . roughly half an hour."

Emerald smirked. "Wow, are you two . . . **an item?**"

"We are," Ophelia said, flashing a smile. "I asked him this evening!"

I looked at the so-called **items,** thoroughly confused. "Can someone explain this item thing to me? This guy named **S** once asked Breeze if **we were an item.**"

"Then maybe you **are,**" Emerald said with a **wink.** "To be certain, you might want to ask her."

"Ask **what?!** What does it even mean?!"

"We'll see you at the dance," Ophelia said with **a smile,** and the two **"items"** bowed and climbed back down the ladder.

"Same for us," Kolb said, meaning him and Emerald. "Or would you care to **walk with us?"**

Breeze shook her head. **"No.** We'll see you there."

"Understood," he winked.

"Don't be late," Emerald said. **"Tonight, you're the stars of the show!"**

As they went down the ladder, I turned to Breeze. "Why didn't you want to walk **with them?"**

"We still have a few minutes, **don't we?"**

"We do." I approached the edge of the tower. "So . . . this is it. **We'll be off soon. . . ."** I gazed at the countless lights below, all the torches that had been replaced, and all the streets and houses along with the wall, still recognizable despite **the damage.** "I'm going to **miss** this place."

"We'll always come back during the holidays."

"I know."

"After we complete our **training,"** Breeze said, "I'd like to join **a guild."**

"What's a guild?"

"They're kind of like clans. There are so many different ones. Maybe we could join one together someday. It'd be fun."

Suddenly, a blue star appeared on the horizon, much brighter than all the rest, the same pale shade of a sea lantern. It grew so bright that it was like a second moon, or the night's version of the sun, nowhere near as bright yet purely beautiful, casting soft light on the mountains beneath—a jagged blue outline. It took me a second to realize what it really was.

"Pebble made it," I said. "He actually lit the beacon."

"I always knew he would." She joined me at the edge of the tower. "Once it's lit, the temple is protected. Forever. That means it's no longer the biggest priority for the Eyeless One. Now we are. More monsters will be searching for us. Before we leave, we'll need to disguise ourselves. We can use the process I mentioned earlier. And . . . my father still has a few enchanted name tags. . . ."

"A new identity? Never liked this name, anyway." I turned to her. "And no matter who we become, we will always be an item."

When she met my eyes, I was reminded that this world is so much more than farms and walls. "I suppose we are." She smirked.

"And a **legendary** one."

To **everyone** who may be reading a copy of my diary: Breeze suggested I **take my journal writing** to the **next level,** in the form of **"archives."** I **agree!** If I'm supposed to record everything that happens in **our world,** I should be a bit more **professional,** right? But don't worry. It won't be **too different**—just a change in **the narration.**

On the plus side, there will be some sections that focus more on **my friends.** I'm sure **you're dying** to know more about Breeze and the others, right? And maybe Stump can even share a few of his advanced crafting recipes!

Stay tuned!

Cube Kid is the pen name of Erik Gunnar Taylor, a writer who has lived in Alaska his whole life. A big fan of video games—especially Minecraft—he discovered early that he also had a passion for writing fan fiction. Cube Kid's unofficial Minecraft fan fiction series, *Diary of a Wimpy Villager*, came out as e-books in 2015 and immediately met with great success in the Minecraft community. They were published in France by 404 éditions in paperback with illustrations by Saboten and now return in this same format to Cube Kid's native country under the title *Diary of an 8-Bit Warrior*. When not writing, Cube Kid likes to travel, putter with his car, devour fan fiction, and play his favorite video game.

Follow your favorite characters in the _new_
Tales of an 8-Bit Kitten series, book I.